When Marnie Was There

The second of four children of barrister parents, Joan G. Robinson spent her early childhood in Hampstead Garden Suburb. She went to seven schools, but passed no exams. Having always wanted to be an illustrator, she began with fourteen books for small children, and later moved on to older children's fiction. She was married to artist and illustrator Richard G. Robinson, and became internationally renowned for her *Teddy Robinson* books, which she began illustrating and writing in 1953. Teddy Robinson was based on her daughter Deborah's own teddy bear – she herself had never had a teddy bear as a child.

When Marnie Was There was shortlisted for the Carnegie Medal in 1968. Joan's fiction was always about girls who felt unloved – and she used to say of *When Marnie Was There*, "You can write books, but there's only ever one book that's really you."

First published in Great Britain by Collins in 1967
First published as a Collins Modern Classic in 2002
This edition published by HarperCollins *Children's Books* in 2014

7 9 10 8 6

HarperCollins *Children's Books* is an imprint of
HarperCollins *Publishers* Ltd, 77-85 Fulham Palace Road, Hammersmith, London W6 8JB

www.harpercollins.co.uk

Text copyright © Joan G. Robinson 1967
Postscript copyright © Deborah Sheppard 2002, 2014
Illustrations by Peggy Fortnum

Joan G. Robinson asserts the moral right to be identified as the author of this work.

ISBN 978-0-00-759135-0

Printed and bound in England by Clays Ltd, St Ives plc

Conditions of Sale
This book is sold subject to the condition that it shall not,
by way of trade or otherwise, be lent, re-sold, hired out or
otherwise circulated without the publisher's prior consent in any form,
binding or cover other than that in which it is published and without
a similar condition including this condition being imposed
on the subsequent purchaser. All rights reserved.

MIX
Paper from
responsible sources
FSC C007454

FSC™ is a non-profit international organisation established to promote
the responsible management of the world's forests. Products carrying the
FSC label are independently certified to assure consumers that they come
from forests that are managed to meet the social, economic and
ecological needs of present and future generations,
and other controlled sources.

Find out more about HarperCollins and the environment at
www.harpercollins.co.uk/green

When Marnie Was There

Joan G. Robinson

Illustrated by Peggy Fortnum

HarperCollins *Children's Books*

CONTENTS

Chapter One

ANNA

MRS PRESTON, WITH her usual worried look, straightened Anna's hat.

"Be a good girl," she said. "Have a nice time and – and – well, come back nice and brown and happy." She put an arm round her and kissed her goodbye, trying to make her feel warm and safe and wanted.

But Anna could feel she was trying and wished she would not. It made a barrier between them so that it was impossible for her to say goodbye naturally, with the spontaneous hug and kiss that other children managed so easily, and that Mrs Preston would so much have liked. Instead she could only stand there stiffly by the open door of the carriage, with her case in her hand, hoping she looked ordinary and wishing the train would go.

Mrs Preston, seeing Anna's 'ordinary' look – which in her own mind she thought of as her 'wooden face' – sighed and turned her attention to more practical things.

"You've got your big case on the rack and your comic's in your mac pocket." She fumbled in her handbag. "Here you are, dear. Some chocolate for the journey and a packet of paper hankies to wipe your mouth after."

A whistle blew and a porter began slamming the carriage doors. Mrs Preston poked Anna gently in the back. "Better get in, dear. You're just off." And then, as Anna scrambled up with a mumbled, "Don't push!" and stood looking down, still unsmiling, from the carriage window – "Give my love to Mrs Pegg and Sam and tell them I'll hope to get down before very long – if I can get a day excursion, that is—" The train began moving imperceptibly along the platform and Mrs Preston began gabbling – "Send me a card when you get there. Remember they're meeting you at Heacham. Don't forget to look out for them. And don't forget to change at King's Lynn, you can't go wrong. There's a stamped card already addressed in the inner pocket of your case. Just to say you've arrived safely – you know. Goodbye, dear, be a good girl."

Then, as she began running and looking suddenly pathetic, almost beseeching, something softened inside Anna just in time. She leaned out of the window and shouted, "Goodbye, Auntie. Thank you for the chocolate. Goodbye!"

She just had time to see Mrs Preston's worried look change to a smile at hearing the unaccustomed use of the name "Auntie", then the train gathered speed and a bend in the line hid her from view.

Anna sat down without looking round, broke off four squares of chocolate, put the rest of the bar in her pocket with the packet of paper handkerchiefs, and opened her comic. Two hours – more than two hours – to King's Lynn. With luck, if she just looked 'ordinary' no-one would speak to her in all that time. She could read her comic and then stare out of the window, thinking about nothing.

Anna spent a great deal of her time thinking about nothing these days. In fact it was partly because of her habit of thinking about nothing that she was travelling up to Norfolk now, to stay with Mr and Mrs Pegg. That – and other things. The other things were difficult to explain, they were so vague and indeterminate. There was the business of not having best friends at school like all the others, not particularly wanting to ask anyone home to tea, and not particularly caring that no-one asked her.

Mrs Preston just would not believe that Anna did not mind. She was always saying things like, "There now, what a shame! Do you mean to say they've all gone off to the ice rink and never asked you?" (Or the cinema, or the Zoo, or the nature ramble, or the treasure hunt.) – And, "Why don't you ask next time? Let them know you'd like to go too. Say something like, 'If you've room for an extra one, how about me? I'd love to come.' If you don't *look* interested nobody'll know you are."

But Anna was not interested. Not any more. She knew perfectly well – though she could never have explained it to Mrs Preston – that things like parties and best friends and going to tea with people were fine for everyone else, because everyone else was 'inside' – inside some sort of invisible magic circle. But Anna herself was outside. And so these things had nothing to do with her. It was as simple as that.

Then there was not-even-trying. That was another thing. Anna always thought of not-even-trying as if it were one long word, she had heard it said so often during the last six months. Miss Davison, her form teacher, said it at school, "Anna, you're not-even-trying." It was written on her report at the end of term. And Mrs Preston said it at home.

"It isn't as if there's anything wrong with you," she would say. "I mean you're not handicapped in any way and I'm sure you're just as clever as any of the others. But this not-even-trying is going to spoil your whole future." And when anyone asked about Anna, which school she would be going to later on, and so on, she would say, "I really don't know. I'm afraid she's not-even-trying. It's going to be difficult to know quite *what* to do with her."

Anna herself did not mind. As with the other things, she was not worried at all. But everyone else seemed worried. First Mrs Preston, then Miss Davison, and then Dr Brown who was called in when she had asthma and couldn't go to school for nearly two weeks.

"I hear you've been worried about school," Dr Brown had remarked with a kindly twinkle in his eye.

"*I'm* not. She is," Anna had mumbled.

"A-ah!" Dr Brown had walked about the bedroom, picking things up and examining them closely, then putting them down again. "And you feel sick before Arithmetic?"

"Sometimes."

"A-ah!" Dr Brown placed a small china pig carefully back on the mantelpiece and stared earnestly into its painted black eyes. "I think you are worried, you know," he murmured. Anna was silent. "Aren't you?" He turned round to face her again.

"I thought you were talking to the pig," she said.

Dr Brown had almost smiled then, but Anna had continued to look severe, so he went on seriously. "I think perhaps you are worried, and I'll tell you why. I think you're worried because your—" He broke off and came towards her again. "What do you call her?"

"Who?"

"Mrs Preston. Do you call her Auntie?" Anna nodded. "I think perhaps you're worried because Auntie's worried, is that it?"

11

"No, I told you, *I'm* not worried."

He had stopped walking about then and stood looking down at her consideringly as she lay there, wheezing, with her 'ordinary' face on. Then he had looked at his watch and said briskly, "Good. Well, that's all right then, isn't it?" and gone running downstairs to talk to Mrs Preston.

After that things changed quite quickly. Firstly Anna didn't go back to school, though it was a good six weeks till the end of term. Instead she and Mrs Preston went shopping and bought shorts and sandshoes and a thick rolltop jersey for Anna. Then Mrs Preston had a reply to the letter she had written to her old friend, Susan Pegg, saying yes, the little lass could come and welcome. She and Sam would be glad to have her, though not so young as they was and Sam's rheumatics something chronic last winter. But seeing she was a quiet little thing and not over fond of gadding about, they hoped she'd be happy. "As you may recall," wrote Mrs Pegg, "we're plain and homely up at ours, but comfortable beds and nothing wanting now we've got the telly."

"Why does she says 'up at ours'?" asked Anna.

"It means at home, at our place. That's how they say it in Norfolk."

"Oh."

Anna had then, surprisingly, slammed the door and stamped noisily upstairs.

"Now whatever did I say to upset her?" thought Mrs

Preston, as she put the letter in the sideboard drawer to show to Mr Preston later. She could never have guessed, but Anna had taken sudden and unreasonable exception to being called "a quiet little thing". It was one thing not to want to talk to people, but quite another to be called names like that. The stamps on the stairs were to prove that she was nothing of the sort.

Remembering this now as she sat in the train pretending to read her comic (which she had long since finished), she suddenly wondered if anyone here might be having the same idea about her. Creasing her forehead into a forbidding frown, she lifted her head for the first time and glared round at the other occupants of the carriage. One, an old man, was fast asleep in a corner. A woman opposite him was making her face up carefully in a pocket mirror. Anna stared, fascinated, for a moment, realised her frown was slipping, and turned to glare at the woman opposite her. She, too, was asleep.

So the 'ordinary' face had worked. No-one had even noticed her. Relieved, she turned to the window and stared out at the long flat stretches of the fens, with their single farmhouses standing isolated from each other, fields apart, and thought about nothing at all.

Chapter Two

THE PEGGS

ANNA KNEW THAT the large, round-faced woman waving a shopping bag at her on the platform must be Mrs Pegg, and went up to her.

"There you are, my duck! Now ain't that nice! And the bus just come in now. Here, give me your case and we'll run!"

A single-decker bus, already nearly full, was waiting in the station yard. "There's a seat down there," panted Mrs Pegg. "Go you on down, my duck, and I'll sit here by the driver. Morning, Mr Beales! Morning Mrs Wells! Lovely weather we're having. And how's Sharon?"

Anna pushed her way down the bus, glad she was not going to have to sit by Sharon, who was only about four and had fat, red-brown cheeks and almost white fair hair. She never knew what to say to children who were so much younger than she was.

Fields stretched on either side, sloping fields of yellow, green and brown. Ploughed fields that looked like brown corduroy, and cabbage fields that were pure blue. As the bus dashed along narrow lanes Anna saw splashes of scarlet poppies in the hedgerows, and then away to the left, she saw the long thin line of the sea. She felt her heart jump and looked around quickly to see whether anyone else had noticed, but no-one had. They were all talking. They must be so used to it that they didn't even see it, she thought, staring and staring… and sank into a quiet dream of nothing, with her eyes wide open.

And then they were at Little Overton. The bus went down a long steep hill, Anna saw a great expanse of sky and sea and sunlit marsh all spread out before her, then the bus turned sharply and drew up with a jolt.

"Not far now," said Mrs Pegg as they picked up the cases and the bus roared away down the coast road. "Sam'll be expecting us now. He'll have heard the bus go by."

"Buses go by all the time at home," said Anna.

"That must be noisy," said Mrs Pegg, clicking her tongue.

"I don't notice it," said Anna. Then remembering the people on the bus, she asked abruptly, "Do you notice it when you see the sea?"

Mrs Pegg looked surprised. "Me see the sea? Oh no, I never do that! I ain't been near-nor-by the sea, not since I were a wench."

"But we saw it from the bus."

"Oh, that! Yes, I suppose you would."

They turned in at a little gate no higher than Anna's hand. The tiny garden was full of flowers and there was a loud humming of bees. They walked up the short path to the open cottage door.

"Here we are, Sam, safe and sound!" said Mrs Pegg, shouting into the darkness, and Anna realised that the large patch of shadow in the corner must be an armchair with Mr Pegg in it. "But we'll take these things up first," said Mrs Pegg, and hustled her into what looked at first sight like a cupboard, but turned out to be a small, steep, winding staircase. At the top she pushed open a door, which opened with a latch instead of a handle. "Here we are. It ain't grand but nice and clean, and a good feather mattress. Come you on down when you're ready, my duck. I'll go and put kettle on."

Anna saw a little room with white walls, a low sloping ceiling, and one small window, so low down in the wall that she had to bend down to see out of it. It looked out on to a small whitewashed yard and an outhouse with a long tin bath hanging on its wall. Beyond that there were fields.

There was a picture over the bed, a framed sampler in red and blue cross-stitch, with the words *Hold fast that which is Good* embroidered over a blue anchor. Anna looked at this with mistrust. It was the word "good". Not that she herself was particularly naughty, in fact her school reports quite often gave her a "Good" for Conduct, but in some odd way the word seemed to leave her outside. She didn't *feel* good...

Still, it was a nice room, she decided cautiously. Plain but nice. Best of all it had the same smell as she had noticed downstairs. A warm, sweet, old smell – quite different from the smell of polish at home or the smell of disinfectant at school.

She hung up her mackintosh on the peg behind the door, then stood for a moment in the middle of the room, holding her breath and listening. She did not want to go down again but there was no excuse for not. She counted six, gave a little cough, and went.

"Ah, so there you are, my biddy!" said Mr Pegg, peering up at her. "My word, but you've growed! Quite a big little-old-girl you're getting to be. Ain't she, Susan?"

Anna looked into Mr Pegg's wrinkled, weatherbeaten face. The small pale blue eyes were almost hidden under shaggy eyebrows.

"How do you do?" she said gravely, holding out her hand.

"A-ah, that's my biddy," said Mr Pegg, taking her hand and patting it absent-mindedly. "And how's your foster-ma keeping, eh?"

Anna looked at Mrs Pegg.

"Your mum, my duck," said Mrs Pegg quickly. "Sam's asking if she's well."

"My mother's dead," said Anna stiffly. "She died ages ago. I thought you knew."

"Yes, yes, my maid. We knowed all about that," said Sam, gruffly kind. "And your gran too, more's the pity." – Anna's face stiffened even more – "That's why I said your foster-ma – Mrs Preston. Nancy Piggott as she used to be. She's your foster-ma, ain't she? A good woman, Nancy Preston. Always had a kind heart. She's a good ma to you, I'll be bound. Keeping nicely, is she?"

18

"She's very well, thank you," said Anna primly.

"But you don't like me calling her 'ma,' eh? Is that it?" said Sam, his eyes crinkling up at the corners.

"No, of course she don't!" said Mrs Pegg. "Ma's old fashioned these days. I expect you call her 'Mum', don't you, love?"

"I call her 'Auntie'," said Anna, then mumbled as an afterthought, "sometimes." It was difficult to know how to explain that she seldom called Mrs Preston by any name at all. There was no need, it wasn't as if there was a crowd of them at home. Only Mr Preston, who called his wife Nan, and occasionally Raymond, who worked in a bank now he was grown up and always called his mother "Mims", or occasionally "Ma" to be funny. Anna thought "Mims" was a silly name to call your own mother... She stood there now in front of Mr Pegg's chair, her eyes troubled, wondering what to say next.

Mrs Pegg came to the rescue. "Any road, I'm sure she's as good as a mother to you, whatever you call her," she said in her downright, comfortable way. "And I'm sure when all's said and done you love her almost as much as if she was your own mother, don't you?"

"Oh, yes!" said Anna. "More," and felt a sudden pricking behind the eyelids as she remembered her last sight of Mrs Preston running to keep up with the train and reminding her about the postcard.

"That's right, then," said Mrs Pegg.

"I've got a postcard to post," said Anna, her voice coming out suddenly loud – she had been so afraid of it cracking – "will you show me where to post it when I've written it?"

Mrs Pegg said yes, of course she would. Anna could write it now in the front room while she got tea ready. "Come you here," she said, "and I'll show you." She wiped her hands down the side of her dress and showed Anna to a room on the other side of the passage. "There's a little table in here under the windie."

The tiny room, over-full of furniture, was in half darkness. Mrs Pegg pulled back the curtains and moved a potted palm from the small bamboo table. Then she bent admiringly over a large white bowl full of pink and blue artificial flowers, which half filled the window.

"Wonderful, ain't they?" she said, blowing the dust from the plastic petals. "Everlasting."

She gazed at them for a moment, wiping the scalloped edges of the boat-shaped bowl with a corner of her dress, then smiled at Anna and went out, closing the door behind her.

This must be the best room, thought Anna, as she tiptoed carefully over the polished linoleum and slippery hearthrug; like the lounge at home, which was only used at weekends or when there were visitors. But very different.

She sat down at the bamboo table and brought out her postcard addressed to *Mrs Stanley Preston, 25 Elmwood Terrace, London*, and wrote on the other side, *Arrived safely. It's quite nice here. My room has a sloping ceiling and the window is on the floor.*

*It smells different from home. I forgot to ask can I wear shorts
every day unless I'm going somewhere special?*

She paused, suddenly wanting to say something more
affectionate than the conventional "love from Anna", but
not knowing how to say it.

From the kitchen came the low rumble of voices. Mrs Pegg
was saying to Sam, "Poor little-old-thing, losing her mother
when she was such a mite – *and* her granny. It's a pity she's
so pale and scrawny, and a bit sober-sides as well, but I expect
we'll rub along together all right. She's taking her time over
that postcard, ain't she? Had I better tell her tea's ready?"

In the front room Anna was still sucking her pen.
Outside, beyond the great boat-shaped bowl that nearly
filled the window ledge, she could see glimpses of the
tiny garden dreaming in the sunshine, bees still buzzing
in and out of the bright flowers. Inside, as imprisoned
as the bluebottles that crawled up and down inside the
closed window, she sat staring at the plastic hydrangeas,
wondering how to tell Mrs Preston that of course she loved
her, without committing herself.

By the time Mrs Pegg had come to the front-room
door and said, "Tea's ready, lass!" she had decided on
"tons of love" instead of just "love", and added a P.S. *The
chocolate was lovely. I've saved some for tonight.*

That, she knew, would please Mrs Preston without
seeming to promise anything. After all, she still might not
always feel loving when she got home again.

Chapter Three

ON THE STAITHE

"JUST UP THE lane and turn left at the crossroads," said Mrs Pegg. "Post Office is only a little way up. And the road to the creek's on the right. Go you and have a look round." She nodded encouragingly and turned back indoors.

Anna found the Post Office – which to her surprise was a cobbled cottage like the Peggs', with a flat letterbox in the wall – and posted her card. Then she walked back to the crossroads. She felt free now. Free and empty. No need to talk to anyone, or be polite, or bother about anything. There was hardly anyone about anyway. A farm worker passed her on a bicycle, said "Good afternoon," and was gone before she even had time to show her surprise. She gave a little skip and turned down the short road to the staithe, and saw the creek lying ahead of her.

There was a salty smell in the air, and from the marsh on the far side of the water came the cries of seabirds. Several small boats were lying at anchor, bumping gently as the tide turned. In that short distance she seemed to have come on another world. A remote, quiet world where there were only boats and birds and water, and an enormous sky.

She jumped at the sudden sound of children's voices. There was laughter, and shouts of, "Come on! They're waiting!" and a group of children appeared round the corner of the staithe. Five or six boys and girls of different ages in navy blue jeans and jerseys. Immediately Anna drew herself up stiffly and put on her 'ordinary' face.

But it was all right, they were not coming her way. They ran, shouting and jostling each other to a car drawn up at the end of the road, and climbed in. Then the doors slammed, the car reversed, and as it drove past her up to the crossroads she had a glimpse of a man at the wheel, a woman beside him, and the children all bobbing about in the back, talking excitely.

It was very quiet when they had gone.

"I'm glad," she said to herself. "I'm glad they've gone. I've met enough new people for one day." But the feeling of freedom had changed imperceptibly to one of loneliness. She knew that even if she had met them they would never have been friends. They were children who were 'inside' – anyone could see that. Anyway, I don't *want* to meet any more people today, she repeated to herself – hardly realising that Mr and Mrs Pegg were the only people she had spoken to since she left London.

And that had been only this morning! Already the turmoil of Liverpool Street Station, the hurry, the confusion, the nearness of parting – against which she had only been able to protect herself with her wooden face – seemed a hundred years ago, she thought.

She listened to the water lapping against the sides of the boats with a gentle slap-slapping sound, and wondered who the boats belonged to. Lucky people, she supposed. Families who came to Little Overton for their holidays year after year and weren't just sent here to be got out of the way, or because of not-even-trying, or because people "didn't quite know what they were going to do with them"… Boys and girls in navy blue jeans and jerseys, like that family…

She walked down to the water's edge, took off her shoes and socks, and stood with her feet in the water, staring out across the marsh. On the horizon lay a line of sandhills, golden where the sun just caught them, and on either side the blue line of the sea. A small bird flew over the creek, quite close to her head, uttering a short plaintive cry four or five times running, all on one note. It sounded like "Pity me! Oh, pity me!"

She stood there looking and listening and thinking about nothing, drinking in the great quiet emptiness of marsh and water and sky, which now seemed to match her own small emptiness inside. Then she turned quickly and looked behind her. She had an odd feeling suddenly that she was being watched.

But there was no-one to be seen. There was no-one on the staithe, nor on the high grassy bank that ran along to the corner of the road. The one or two cottages appeared to be empty, and the door of the boathouse was shut. To the right the village straggled away into fields, and in the distance a windmill stood alone, silhouetted against the sky.

She turned and looked away to the left. Beyond the few cottages a long brick wall ran along the grassy bank, ending in a clump of dark trees.

And then she saw the house...

As soon as she saw it Anna knew that this was what she had been looking for. The house, which faced straight on to the creek, was large and old and square, its many small windows framed in faded blue woodwork. No wonder she had felt she was being watched with all those windows staring at her!

This was no ordinary house, in a long road, like the

one she lived in at home. This house stood alone, and had a quiet, mellow, everlasting look, as if it had been there so long, watching the tide rise and fall, and rise and fall again, that it had forgotten the busyness of life going on ashore behind it, and had sunk into a quiet dream. A dream of summer holidays, and sandshoes littered about the ground-floor rooms, dried strips of seaweed still flapping from an upper window where some child had hung them as a weather indicator, and shrimping nets in the hall, and small buckets, a dried starfish swept into a corner, an old sun hat…

All these things Anna sensed as she stood staring at the house. And yet none of them had she ever known. Or had she…? Once, when she was in the Home, she had been to the seaside with all the other children, but she hardly remembered that. And twice she and the Prestons had been to Bournemouth and walked along the promenade and sat in the flower gardens. They had bathed too, and sat in deck chairs, and been to the concert party at nights.

But this was different. Here there was none of the gay life of Bournemouth. It was as if the old house had found itself one day on the staithe at Little Overton, looked across at the stretch of water with the marsh behind, and the sea beyond that, and had settled down on the bank, saying, "I like this place. I shall stay here for ever." That was how it looked, Anna thought, gazing at it with a sort of longing. Safe and everlasting.

She paddled along in the water until she was directly

opposite to it, and stood, looking and looking... The windows were dark and uncurtained. One of the upper ones was open but no-one was looking out. And yet it seemed to Anna almost as if the house had been expecting her, watching her, waiting for her to turn round and recognise it. And in some way she did.

As she stood there, half dreaming in the water a few feet from the shore, the strange feeling crept over her that this had all happened before. It would have been difficult to explain even what she meant by this, but it was almost as if she were now standing outside of herself, somewhere farther back, watching herself standing there in the water – a small figure in her best blue dress with her socks and shoes in her hand, looking across the staithe at the old house with many windows. She even noticed without concern that the water must have risen slightly, because she could see it lapping at the hem of her dress, making a dark stain round the very edge.

Then the little grey-brown bird flew overhead again, crying, "Pity me! Oh, pity me!" and Anna shook herself out of her dream... She looked down and saw that the water had come up to her knees while she had been standing there. It had even reached the hem of her dress...

"Who lives in the big house by the water?" she asked Mrs Pegg, as they sat drinking cocoa in the kitchen later.

"The big house by the water?" said Mrs Pegg vaguely. "Now which one would that be?"

"The one with blue windows."

Mrs Pegg turned to Sam, who was eating bread and cheese, spearing pickled onions on the end of his knife and putting them whole into his mouth. "Who lives in the big house with the blue windows, Sam?"

Mr Pegg looked equally vague. He thought for a moment, then said, "Oh, ah, you mean The Marsh House? I don't know as anyone lives there, do they, Susan?"

Mrs Pegg shook her head. "Not as I know of, but I never go down by the staithe so I wouldn't know. Didn't I hear it was going to be bought by a London gentleman? I think Miss Manders at Post Office said so. 'That'll need a fair lot of doing up,' she said. 'It's been empty quite a while.' But maybe that's not the one."

"And who are the children in navy blue jeans and jerseys?" asked Anna. "The big family?"

Again Mrs Pegg looked puzzled. "I don't know of none," she said. "In the summer holidays there's lots of children, of course, in their holiday clothes like that. But I don't know of none now, do you, Sam?"

Mr Pegg shook his head. "Maybe they was just down for the day," he suggested helpfully.

"Yes, perhaps," said Anna, remembering the car. But she was secretly disappointed. In her own mind she had already decided that the house by the water was theirs. They had looked the right sort of family to live in a house like that.

"Anything else you'd like to know?" asked Mr Pegg, smiling.

"Yes," said Anna. "Which is the bird that says, 'Pity me! Oh, pity me!'"

Mrs Pegg gave her an odd look. "Time you was in bed, my lass," she said briskly. "It's been a long day, what with the journey and all. Come you on up and I'll get you settled in." She pulled herself out of her chair and carried the cups into the scullery to put them in the sink.

Anna got up and stood looking down at Mr Pegg still eating his bread and cheese. "Goodnight, then," she said.

"Ah, goodnight, my biddy!" he said abstractedly. "I'm thinking – might that be a sandpiper, do you think? That makes a lonesome little cry, that does. Though I can't say I ever heared the words afore!" he added with a chuckle.

Chapter Four

THE OLD HOUSE

ANNA THOUGHT OF the house as soon as she awoke next morning. In fact she must have been thinking about it even before she awoke, because by the time she opened her eyes and saw the white, sloping ceiling of her little room, and smelt the old, sweet, warm smell of the cottage, she was saying to herself – still half asleep – "I must hurry. It's waiting for me." Then she realised where she was.

Thank goodness the journey to Norfolk was over! She must have been dreading it more than she had realised. It had been an unknown adventure looming up ahead, and all her life at home during the past few weeks had been a preparation for it. Now it was over. She was here. And as soon as she could she would go down to the creek again and see the house.

At breakfast Mrs Pegg said, "How about coming into Barnham with me on the bus? I usually goes once a week to the shops, and it would make something for you, wouldn't it, lass?"

Anna looked doubtful.

"Or maybe you'd like to play with young Sandra-up-at-the-Corner?" Mrs Pegg suggested. "She's a well behaved, nicely-spoken little lass. I know her mum and I could take you up there."

Anna looked more doubtful still.

Had she noticed the windmill yesterday, Sam asked. It was a fair way off, and not much to look at when you got there, but that might make something too.

Mrs Pegg rounded on him. That would do nothing of the sort, she said. It was too far for the lass on her own and all along the main road into the bargain.

"Oh, ah, so it is!" said Sam. "Never mind, my biddy. Maybe I'll take you there myself one day."

Anna said she did not mind at all, she was quite all right doing nothing. "Really I like doing nothing better than anything else," she explained earnestly. They both laughed at this, but Anna, determined to be taken seriously, stared hard at the tablecloth, looking as ordinary as she knew how.

"I don't know that I can do with you sitting around in the kitchen all day, my duck," Mrs Pegg said doubtfully. "What with the cleaning and the cooking and the washing and Sam being under my feet half the time as it is—"

Anna interrupted. "Oh, no! I meant outside. Can I go down to the creek?"

Mrs Pegg looked relieved. She had been afraid Anna might have wanted to spend the day in the front room, the door of which was always kept closed except on special occasions. Yes, of course Anna could go down to the creek. Or if the tide was out she could walk over the marsh to the beach, and if it was high she could always go down in Wuntermenny's boat. "As long as you don't mind not having no company," she said. Anna assured her she did not mind.

"And just as well, if you go down in the boat with Wuntermenny West," said Sam. "He can't abide having to talk." He stirred his tea ponderously with the handle of his fork and looked hopefully across the table at her. "No doubt you're thinking that's a queer name, eh?" he said, smiling.

Anna had not thought about it but said, "Yes," politely.

"Ah! I'll tell you how it was, then, since you're asking," said Sam. "Wuntermenny's ma – old Mrs West, that was – she had ten already when he was born. 'What're you going to call him, mam?' they all says, and she says, tired-like, 'Lord knows! He'm one-too-many and *that's* a fact.' So that's how

32

it was!" he said, laughing and spluttering into his mug of tea. "And Wuntermenny West he's been ever since."

As soon as she could get away, Anna ran down to the staithe. The tide was out and the creek had dwindled to a mere stream. At first she was disappointed when she saw the old house again. It seemed to have lost some of its magic, now that it only looked out on to a littered foreshore instead of a wide stretch of water. But even as she looked, she saw that it was still the same quiet, friendly-faced house. She felt rather as if she had come to visit an old friend, and found that friend asleep.

She scrambled up the bank, clinging on to tufts of grass, and walked slowly along the footpath in front of the house, looking sideways into the windows. She was not sure if she was trespassing, and it was difficult to see clearly without stopping and pressing her face up close against the glass. Suppose someone should be watching, from inside! More than ever now she had the feeling she was spying on someone who was asleep. She moved nearer and saw only her own face staring back at her, pale and wide-eyed.

The Peggs were right, she thought. No-one was living in the house. Nevertheless, it still had a faintly lived-in look, more as if it were waiting for its people to return, than having been deserted. She grew bolder and looked through the narrow side windows on either side of the front door. There was a lamp on a windowsill, and a torn shrimping net was leaning up against the wall. She saw that a wide central staircase went up from the middle of the hall.

That was all there was to see. She slid down the bank again, waded across the creek, and sat for a long time with her chin in her hands, staring across at the house, and thinking about nothing. If Mrs Preston had known she would have been even more worried than she had been, but at the moment she was more than a hundred miles away, pushing a wire trolley round the supermarket. She had forgotten that in a place like Little Overton you can think about nothing all day long without anyone noticing.

Anna did go down to the beach in Wuntermenny's boat. She found him as unsociable as the Peggs had promised. He was small and bent, with a thin, lined face, and eyes which seemed to be permanently screwed up against the light, looking into the far distance. After the first grunt of recognition he hardly noticed her, so she was able to sit up in the bow of the boat, looking ahead, and ignore him too. This suited her well, but it made her feel lonelier, and she was a little frightened that first afternoon. There seemed such a huge expanse of water and sky, and so little of herself.

Sitting alone on the shore, while Wuntermenny in the far distance was digging for bait, she looked back at the long, low line of the village and tried to pick out The Marsh House. But it was not there! She could see the boathouse, and the white cottage at the corner, and farther away still she could see the windmill. But along where The

Marsh House should have been there was only a bluish-grey smudge of trees.

Alarmed, she stood up. It *had* to be there. If it was not, then nothing seemed safe any more... nothing made sense... She blinked, opened her eyes wider, and looked again. Still it was not there. She sat down then – with the most ordinary face in the world, to show she was quite independent and not frightened at all – and with her knees up to her chin, and her arms round her knees, made herself into as small and tight a parcel as she could, until Wuntermenny came trudging up the beach with his fork and his bucket of bait.

"Cold?" he grunted, when he saw her.

"No."

She followed him down to the boat, and those were the only two words that passed between them all the afternoon. But as they rounded a bend in the creek and she saw the old house gradually emerge from its dark background of trees, she felt so hot and happy with relief that she nearly said, "There it is!" out loud. She realised now that it had been there all the time. In the distance the old brick and blue-painted woodwork had merely merged into the blue-green of the thick garden trees. She realised something else, too. As they passed close under the windows, on the high tide, she saw that the house was no longer asleep. Again it had a watching, waiting look, and again she had the feeling it had recognised her and was glad she was coming back.

"Enjoy yourself?" asked Mrs Pegg, who was frying sausages and onions in the scullery when Anna returned.

Anna nodded.

"That's right, my duck. You do what you like. Just suit yourself and follow your fancy."

"And maybe I'll take you along to the windmill one day if you're a good lass," said Sam.

Chapter Five

ANNA FOLLOWS HER FANCY

SO THAT WAS how it was. Anna suited herself and went where she liked. In a way, now, she had three different worlds in Little Overton. The world of the Peggs' cottage, small and warm and cosy. The world of the staithe, where the boats swung at anchor in the creek and The Marsh House watched for her out of its many windows. And the world of the beach, where great gulls swooped overhead and she sometimes found rabbit burrows in the sand dunes, and the bones of porpoises lying in the fine, white sand. Three separate worlds… but in her own mind the important one was the staithe with the old house by the water.

Gradually, instead of thinking about nothing, she thought about The Marsh House nearly all the time; imagining the family who would live there, what it was like inside, and how it would look in the evenings, in autumn, with the curtains drawn and a big fire blazing in the hearth.

Trudging home across the marsh at sunset one evening she saw the windows all lit up and ran, thinking they must have arrived while she was down at the beach. Perhaps if she hurried she might catch sight of them – the family of children in navy blue jeans and jerseys – before the curtains were pulled. But as she drew nearer she saw that she was wrong. There were no lights in the house. It had only been the reflection of the sunset in the windows.

On another day she saw – or thought she saw – a face pressed close to the window; a girl's face with long, fair hair hanging down on either side – watching. Then it disappeared. Even when there was clearly no-one there, she still had this curious feeling of being watched. She grew used to it.

The Peggs were glad she had settled down so well. It was good for the lass to be out of doors so much, and provided she came in to meals at reasonable hours, and ate heartily, they saw nothing to worry about. She was, in fact, "no trouble at all," as Mrs Pegg assured Miss Manders at the Post Office.

A letter came from Mrs Preston in answer to Anna's card. She was glad Anna was happy, and yes she could wear the shorts every day as long as Mrs Pegg didn't mind. *We're looking forward so much to hearing all the interesting things you're doing,* she wrote, *but if you haven't time for a long letter, a card will do.* Enclosed was a small folded note with "Burn this" written across the outside, and inside, *Does the house really smell, dear? Tell me what sort of smell.*

Anna, who had quite forgotten her remark about the cottage smelling different from home, wondered vaguely what it meant, burnt the note obediently, and forgot about it. She bought a postcard with a picture of a kitten in a flower pot on it, and wrote on the back, *I'm sorry I didn't write before but I forgot, and on Thursday the Post Office was shut so I couldn't buy this card. I hope you like it.* There was only room for one more line, so she put, *I went to the beach. Love from Anna.* She added two Xs for good measure, and posted it, well satisfied, never dreaming Mrs Preston might be disappointed at having so little news.

One day Sandra-up-at-the-Corner came to the cottage with her mother. Dinner was late that day, so Anna was caught before she had time to slip out of the scullery door.

Sandra was fair and solid. Her dress was too short and her knees were too fat, and she had nothing to say. Anna spent a wretched afternoon playing cards with her at the kitchen table, while Mrs Pegg and Sandra's mother sat and talked in the front room. Sandra and Anna knew different versions of every game, Sandra cheated, and they had nothing to talk about.

In the end Anna pushed all her cards over to Sandra's side and said, "Here you are. Keep them all, then you'll be sure to win."

Sandra said, "Ooh, *that* I never!" went bright pink and relapsed into sulks in the rocking chair. She spent the rest of the afternoon examining the lace edge of her nylon petticoat, and trying to twist her straight, straw-coloured hair into ringlets. Anna read Mrs Pegg's *Home Words* in a corner and was thankful when they went.

After that she was less trouble than ever, and stayed out all day in case she might ever have to play with Sandra again.

One afternoon, coming back from the beach where Wuntermenny had been collecting driftwood, and she had been looking for shells, Wuntermenny astonished her by saying his first complete sentence. They were coming up towards the staithe when he suddenly jerked his head over his shoulder and said in a gruff, casual voice, "Reckon they'll be down soon."

Anna sat up in surprise. "Who will?"

Wuntermenny jerked his head again, over towards the shore. "Them as've took The Marsh House."

"*Will* they? When? Who are they?"

Wuntermenny gave her a look of deep, pitying scorn and shut his mouth tightly. Too late she realised her mistake. She had been too eager, asked too many questions. If she had just looked sleepily uninterested he would probably have told her all she wanted to know. Never mind, she would soon find out. She might even ask the Peggs.

But on second thoughts she decided not. They might think she wanted to make friends with the people, and that was not what she wanted at all. She wanted to know *about* them, not to know them. She wanted to discover, gradually, what their names were, choose which one she thought she might like best, guess what sort of games they played, even what they had for supper and what time they went to bed.

If she really got to know them, and they her, all that would be spoiled. They would be like all the others then – only half friendly. They, from inside, looking curiously at her, outside – expecting her to like what they liked, have what they had, do what they did. And when they found she didn't, hadn't, couldn't – or what ever it was that always cut her off from the rest – they would lose interest. If they then hated her it would have been better. But nobody did. They just lost interest, quite politely. So then she had to hate *them*. Not furiously, but coldly – looking ordinary all the time.

But this family would be different. For one thing they would be living in 'her' house. That in itself set them apart. They would be like her family, almost – so long as she was careful never to get to know them.

So she said nothing to the Peggs about what Wuntermenny had said, and hugged to herself the secret that they would soon be coming to The Marsh House. And as the days went by she followed her fancy in her imagination as well, until the unknown family became almost like a dream family in her own mind – so determined was she that they should not be real.

Chapter Six

"A STIFF, PLAIN THING—"

ONE EVENING ANNA and Wuntermenny were coming
home in the boat on a particularly high tide.

The sky was the colour of peaches, and the water
so calm that every reed and the mast of every boat was
reflected with barely a quiver. The tide was flooding,
covering quite a lot of the marsh, and as they drifted
upstream Anna had been peering down into the water,
watching the sea lavender and the green marsh weed, called
samphire, waving under the surface. Then, as they rounded

the last bend, she turned as she always did, to look towards The Marsh House.

Behind it the sky was turning a pale lime green, and a thin crescent moon hung just above the chimney pot. They drew nearer, and then she saw, quite distinctly, in one of the upper windows, a girl. She was standing patiently, having her hair brushed. Behind her the shadowy figure of a woman moved dimly in the unlighted room, but the girl stood out clearly against the dark, secret square of the window. Anna could even see the long pale strands of her hair lifted now and then as the brush passed over them.

She turned quickly and glanced at Wuntermenny, but he was looking along the staithe towards the landing place and had seen nothing.

Anna ran home, turned the corner of the lane, then stopped. Mrs Pegg and Sandra's mother were standing talking at the cottage gate – their faces brick red in the orange light of the sunset. Mrs Stubbs was a big woman with bright black eyes and a rasping voice. Anna did not want to meet her again, so she stepped back into the dusky shadow of the hedge, and waited.

"You'll be coming over to mine tonight, won't you?" Mrs Stubbs was saying. "My sister's over from Lynn and she's brought them patterns."

"Has she now!" Mrs Pegg sounded eager, then hesitated. "Well, there's the child –" she added doubtfully.

"Oh, I forgot about her! She's a bit of an awkward one, ain't she? My Sandra said—" the voice was lowered and Anna missed the rest of the sentence.

"Yes, well – maybe…" said Mrs Pegg, "but I don't hold with interfering between children. If they don't want to make friends, then let 'em alone, I'd say."

"My Sandra was quite willing," said Mrs Stubbs. "Put on her best dress, she did, *and* her new petticoat, but she says to me after, 'Mum,' she says. 'Never did I see such a stiff, plain thing—'"

"Yes, well," Mrs Pegg interrupted mildly, turning towards the gate, "don't tell *me* what she said, for as true as I'm standing here, I'd rather not know." She closed the latch with a click. "Any road, she's as good as gold with us," she added – defiantly now she was inside the gate. "But perhaps we won't come tonight and thank you all the same for asking."

"Just as you please," said Mrs Stubbs. "Shall you be at the Bingo tomorrow night?"

"Yes, that's right. I'll see you at the Bingo tomorrow," said Mrs Pegg, and went indoors.

Anna waited until Mrs Stubbs had gone, then slipped in by the back door. Mrs Pegg was bustling about, fetching bread and butter from the pantry. She looked a little flushed and her hair was untidy but she greeted Anna as usual.

"Ah, there you are, lass! Sit you down now. Tea's just ready." She turned to Sam as he put down his paper and drew up a chair. "What's on telly tonight?" she asked.

Sam looked surprised. "Weren't you going up to the Corner tonight? I thought Mrs Stubbs said her sister was there?"

Mrs Pegg shook her head. "Not tonight. That can wait." She glanced at Anna, then said, "Listen, love, next time you see Mrs Stubbs or Sandra, try and be a bit friendly-like, will you?"

Anna blurted out, "Is it because of me you're not going?"

"Of course not, what an idea!" Mrs Pegg made a good pretence of looking surprised. "Only maybe they'll ask you up to theirs one day, if you look friendly-like. That might make a bit of a change for you, eh?"

Anna mumbled, "I like it better here," but Mrs Pegg might not have heard because she was again asking Sam what was on the telly.

"Boxing," he said, looking slightly guilty, "but you won't like that."

"Oh, well," said Mrs Pegg, "I'll like it tonight and lump it. And that'll make a bit of a change too."

"It will and all!" said Sam, chuckling and turning to wink at Anna. "She'll never look at boxing, no matter what I say—" But Anna had gone.

Upstairs in her room she sat on the edge of her bed, hating herself and hating everyone else. It was her fault that Mrs Pegg wasn't going to the Stubbs' tonight. Sandra, that fat pig of a girl, had called her a stiff, plain thing. Mrs Pegg – kind Mrs

Pegg – hadn't wanted to listen and she had said she was as good as gold. But she wasn't going to the Stubbs' because of Anna, and that was *stupid*. She was silly and stupid. So was Sam, with his silly boxing. And as for Mrs Stubbs—! Mrs Pegg should have gone anyway, then Anna wouldn't have felt so guilty. She looked at the framed sampler on the wall and hated that too. *Hold fast that which is Good* – but nothing was good. Anyway what did it mean? Was the anchor supposed to be good? But you couldn't walk about holding an anchor all day long, even if you had one. You'd look sillier than ever.

She turned the picture to the wall and went over to the window. Kneeling on the floor she looked out across the fields, pink in the glow of the sunset, and let hot, miserable tears run down her face. Nothing was any good – Anna least of all.

For a moment she almost wished she was at home, then she remembered all the misery of that last half term before she came away. No, it was better here.

She knelt there, listening to the now familiar country sounds; voices from the fields, the distant rattle of farm machinery, and the roar of the last bus from Barnham as it came tearing down the hill and disappeared along the coast road. Then there was silence – only the odd cry of a bird from the marsh, and little ticking sounds that she could never quite identify. At night the silence fell like a blanket. When a dog barked you could hear it from one end of the village to the other.

Gradually, as the tears dried on her cheeks and the fields darkened, and the quietness became even quieter, she forgot about Mrs Pegg not going to the Stubbs', and thought instead about the girl she had seen in The Marsh House. Why had she been having her hair brushed? It had been too early for bedtime. She had been wearing something light, surely not a nightdress so early in the evening? She had not been a very little girl. She had looked about the same age as Anna...

The thought struck her that the girl would have been dressing for a party. Yes, that was it. She would have been standing there in her petticoat, having her hair brushed, with a white party dress laid out on the bed nearby, and a pair of slippers on the floor – silver slippers. And now, with dusk already falling, she would be coming down the central staircase into the hall. There would be bright lights and there would be dancing...

Kneeling quite still by the open window, Anna sank into a dream, seeing it all as if she herself were there – not inside, but watching from the footpath outside. Through the narrow side window she could see the bright dresses passing and repassing. The faces of the people were vague, but she could tell they were laughing. Then all at once she saw them turn one way, to watch the fair-haired girl as she came down the great staircase, stepping carefully in her silver slippers.

And now, it seemed to Anna, she was farther away. She was standing on the marsh on the far side of the water, and seeing the lights from the windows reflected in the creek, a wavering pattern of gold. The sound of music came over the water, only faintly and mingling with the soughing of the wind in the marram grasses...

So clearly did she see it all in her imagination that she felt it must be true – must be happening now. Getting to her feet she closed the window, then, stiff with kneeling so long, and trembling, partly with cold and partly with excitement, she limped softly across the room and downstairs. As she slipped out of the door she heard the shouts and roars of the television boxing match going on in the kitchen, and marvelled how grown-ups could spend an evening watching anything so dull.

She hurried down to the creek, running barefoot, her ears straining for the sounds of the music, her eyes straining to catch a glimpse of the lights which by now she felt sure would be spreading right across the creek. Then she turned the corner and stopped dead.

The creek was in darkness, the cottages and the boathouse were in darkness, and along where The Marsh House stood, only the black background of trees showed up against the sky. There was not a light anywhere, except for the distant revolving beam of a lightship which made an arc of light across the sky every half minute, then disappeared. There was no music either, only the soft lapping of water against the sides of the boats, and the sudden, feverish rattling of rigging slapping against masts...

She stood there for a moment, amazed. Then from far across the marsh came the mad, scary, scatter-brained cry of a peewit, and she turned and fled back to the cottage.

Chapter Seven

"—AND A FAT PIG"

THAT WAS SILLY, Anna thought next morning. Because she had been miserable about the way things really were, she had tried to make something imaginary come true instead. But that never worked.

She went down to breakfast thinking she would try and make it up to Mrs Pegg for missing her outing, by being helpful in some way.

"Shall I wash up?" she asked casually, standing beside her at the sink after breakfast.

"Lord no, my duck! That's kind of you, but I'm used to it." Mrs Pegg seemed touched, and a little surprised. "I'll tell you what, though. You *can* do something for me. Pick me some sanfer when you're down on the marsh, and on your way back pop in and ask Miss Manders if she's any spare jam jars. If she has, get some vinegar as well. Sam's a fancy to have some pickled sanfer again."

The Peggs always called samphire "sanfer", so Anna knew what she meant. She set off with the big, black plastic shopping bag and went down to the creek.

It was one of those still, grey, pearly days, with no wind, when sky and water seemed to merge into one, and everything was soft and sad and dreamy. Sam had said at breakfast that in weather like this his rheumatics were like Old Nick screwing the pincers on him, but Anna liked these days better than any. They seemed to match the way she was feeling.

The tide was out, and she paddled across to the other side without even turning to look at the old house. There was a purple haze over the marsh, which was the sea lavender coming out, and she thought she might pick some of that, too, when she had finished with the samphire.

For two hours she slithered about on the marsh, jumping over the streams, sometimes landing on springy turf and sometimes sinking into soft patches of black mud; hearing only the distant cry of the little grey-brown birds calling "Pity me! Oh, pity me!" from a long way off. The samphire was green and juicy, though it only tasted of sea salt, she thought. She picked until the bag was full, then, deciding to leave the sea lavender for another day, she set off towards the Post Office.

Miss Manders looked at Anna over her spectacles and gave her a thin, tight smile. Anna gave her Mrs Pegg's message, hearing, at the same time, someone come in behind her. Out of the corner of her eye she saw that it was Sandra and another girl.

"—and Mrs Pegg says if you can spare the jam jars, please can she have some vinegar as well," she finished, aware that the two girls were looking at her sideways and that Sandra was whispering. The younger girl burst into a peal of laughter, then there was some shushing and quiet scuffling behind her.

When Miss Manders had gone out at the back to find the jars, Anna turned round with every intention of looking friendly, if she could. But try as she would she could not catch Sandra's eye. She was now standing with her back to Anna, pretending to look at some postcards in a rack, and talking to her friend in a low voice. Again the other girl laughed, half glancing over her shoulder at Anna. Then Sandra, looking into a crate of ginger beer bottles, said loudly in an affected voice, "Ho, and hif you 'ave any old bottles to spare, kindly fill them with ginger beer, will you?"

They both laughed immoderately at this, and Anna stood there feeling awkward, but she was determined to make Sandra look at her. She walked over towards her, intending to say "Hello," but at that minute Miss Manders came back.

"Tell Mrs Pegg I have got some," she said to Anna, "but I'll have to look them out later. They're away at the back."

Anna said, "Thank you," and moved towards the door. Then she remembered the vinegar. She went back and stood uncertainly behind the two girls, waiting while Miss Manders served them with two ice-cream wafers. Then the telephone rang, and Miss Manders, thinking Anna was only waiting for the others, shut the till and went to answer it. Sandra turned round and faced Anna.

"Why are you following me about?" she demanded.

"I'm not."

"Yes, you are. Wasn't she?"

The other girl nodded, licking delicately round the edges of her ice-cream. Sandra put out her tongue and kept it out, staring hard at Anna, then, very slowly and deliberately, without shifting her gaze, she lifted her ice-cream and ran it down the sides of her tongue.

Anna stared back, noting with pleasure that the ice-cream from the lower end of the wafers was about to dribble down the front of Sandra's dress. But she showed no sign.

"I was only going to say hello—" she began coldly, but Sandra interrupted before she could finish her sentence.

"Go on, then, call me, call me!"

"What do you mean, call you?"

"Call me what you like. *I* don't care! I know what you look like, any road." She turned and whispered to her companion, giggling, and the blob of ice-cream fell trickling down her dress.

Anna looked at her scornfully. "Fat pig," she said, and turned to go out.

But Sandra barred her way. She had just seen the ice-cream on her dress and was scrubbing at it furiously. "Now I'll tell you!" she said, spluttering. "Now I'll tell you what you look like! You look like – like *just what you are*. There!"

This startled Anna. She walked out of the Post Office – quite forgetting the vinegar – with all the appearance of not having heard, but knowing that Sandra had dealt her an underhand blow. Like "*just what you are*" she had said. But what was she?

Angrily she walked down the lane, tearing at the poppies in the hedgerow, and crumpling them in her hot hand until they became slimy. She knew what she was only too well. She was ugly, silly, bad tempered, stupid, ungrateful, rude… and that was why nobody liked her. But to be told so by Sandra! She would never forgive her for that.

She left the bag of samphire behind the outhouse, and went in to dinner looking sulky.

Mrs Pegg did not know yet about her meeting Sandra, but she would hear soon enough. Mrs Stubbs would make sure of that. She would tell her that Anna had called Sandra a fat pig – and this after Mrs Pegg had specially said "try and look friendly"! Anna prepared herself in advance for the moment when Mrs Pegg should hear about it, by looking surly and answering all her kindly questions in monosyllables.

"Ready for your dinner, love?"

"Yes."

"Liver today. Do you like that?"

"Quite."

"What's up, my duck. Got out of bed the wrong side after all, did you?"

"No."

"Never mind, then. You like bacon too – and onions?"

"Yes."

Mrs Pegg hovered beside her with the frying pan. "A please don't hurt no-one neither," she said a little tartly.

"Please," said Anna.

"That's a maid! Now sit you down and enjoy that. Maybe you'll feel better after."

Anna ate her meal in silence, then got up to go. Sam reached out a hand as she passed his chair. "What ails you, my biddy?"

"Nothing."

She ignored the hand, pretending not to see it, but in that instant she longed to flop down on the floor beside him and tell him everything. But she could not have done that without crying, and the very idea of such a thing appalled her. Anyway they would miss the point somehow. Mrs Preston always did. She was always kind, but also she was always so terribly concerned. If only there was someone who would let you cry occasionally for no reason, or hardly any reason at all! But there seemed to be some conspiracy against that. Long ago in the Home, she remembered, it had been the same. She could not remember the details, only a picture of herself running, sobbing across an enormous asphalt playground, and a woman as big as a mountain – as it had seemed to her then – swooping down on her in amazement, crying, "Anna! Anna! What *ever* are you crying for?" As if it had been a quite outrageous thing to do in that happy, happy place.

All this passed through Anna's mind as she passed Sam's chair and went through into the scullery to put her empty plate into the sink. On no account must she cry. It would be too silly to say she was upset because she had called Sandra a fat pig. Or because Sandra had said she looked like just what she was. It was not just that, anyway. Mrs Pegg was going to hate her as soon as she heard about it, so it would be unfair to let her go on being kind now, not knowing.

She hardened her heart and went out by the back door, slamming it behind her.

The tide was far out and the creek a mere trickle. She glanced along the staithe towards The Marsh House, wondering if she might catch a glimpse of the girl she had seen last night, but there was no-one there. The house seemed asleep. She crossed the creek and walked over the marsh, paddling across the creek again on the far side, and came to the beach. There, with only the birds for company, she lay in a hollow in the sandhills all the long, hot afternoon, and thought about nothing.

Chapter Eight

MRS PEGG'S BINGO NIGHT

IT WAS MRS Pegg's Bingo night. Anna had forgotten until she came back several hours later to find Mrs Pegg already changed into her best blouse, and rummaging in the dresser drawer for a small pot of vanishing cream which she kept there for special occasions.

"Your tea's keeping hot over the saucepan," she said to Anna. "Turn off the gas when you've finished, there's a good lass. Sam's up to the Queen's Head for a game of dominoes, so he had his early with me. Now where's that pot of cream gone? It really do seem like vanishing cream sometimes. Ah, there it is!" She pulled it out from among an assortment of kettle holders, paper bags and tea cloths, and began dabbing her face haphazardly. "Now where are me shoes? I could have swore I brought them down. You won't forget to turn the gas off, will you, love? I'd better go and find me shoes." She lumbered off to find another pair.

Anna was glad. No-one had been bothering about her. No-one had been wasting their time worrying whether she was happy or not. Her bad temper of dinner-time had been forgotten. Now Bingo and dominoes were in the ascendant. The Peggs were like that; they really did forget, not just pretend to. So she, too, was free – free to cut herself right off from them. From the Peggs, the Stubbs, and everyone else. It was a relief not to feel she was being watched and worried over all the time... In any case, by tomorrow Mrs Pegg would probably have heard all about her meeting with Sandra... When Mrs Pegg came hobbling back in her best shoes (which were exactly the same as her ordinary ones, only tighter), Anna was looking out of the window. And when Mrs Pegg finally went to the door, saying, "Well, I'm off at last, my duck. Make yourself some tea if you've a mind," she only glanced round and said, "Goodbye" in a polite, formal voice.

And now Anna was alone. The clock ticked on the dresser, and the saucepan on the stove bubbled gently. She discovered her "tea" – a mountain of baked beans alongside a kipper, and a sticky iced bun – and ate through it solemnly, still wrapped around in this quiet, untouchable state of not-caring. Then she turned off the gas, put the dishes on the draining board, and went out again.

It was dusk and the tide had come in. It must have come in very quickly while she was having her tea, for the staithe was now covered with a smooth sheet of silvery water, which came up to within a few feet of the bank. A small boat was tied to a post, floating in shallow water barely a foot from the shore. It had not been there before, she was sure. She could not have failed to notice it lying on its side as it would have been then, and so far up on the beach. It was a beautiful little boat, almost new and the colour of a polished walnut.

She went closer and looked inside.

A silver anchor lay in the bow, its white rope neatly coiled, and a pair of oars were lying ready in the rowlocks. It looked as if someone had just stepped ashore and would be back any minute. She looked round quickly but there was no-one to be seen. Nor had anyone come up the road for at least the last ten minutes. If they had, Anna would have seen them. And yet, more and more, she had the feeling that the boat was waiting for someone; not just lying idle like the others. After all, it was not moored, the anchor was still in the bow, and the rope was only twisted twice round the post. It almost seemed as if it might be waiting for her.

She glanced round again, took off her plimsolls and then, without pausing to think, pulled the boat towards her and stepped inside. The sudden movement tugged at the rope and loosened it. Anna sat down, pulled it in, and took hold of the oars. She had never rowed a boat before in her life – though she did remember once taking an oar with Mr Preston when they had been in Bournemouth, and she remembered, too, the golden rule he had impressed upon her about never standing up in a boat – but beyond that she had no experience at all. And yet now she felt perfectly confident.

Carefully she dipped one oar, then the other, then both together in small quiet strokes, and found herself moving steadily away from the post and along the shore. She was moving along towards The Marsh House. Almost without realising it she had turned the boat in that direction.

It was utterly calm and dreamlike on the water. She forgot to row and leaned forward on the oars, looking at the afterglow of the sunset, which lay in streaks along the horizon. A sandpiper – was it a sandpiper? – called, "Pity me!" from across the marsh, and another answered, "Pity me! Oh, pity me!"

She sat up suddenly, realising that although she had stopped rowing she was still moving. The bank to her left was slipping away fast, and already she was drifting past the front of The Marsh House. She saw lights in the first-floor windows, then she made a sudden grab for the oars. Over her shoulder she had just seen that she was heading straight for the corner where the wall jutted out into the water. If she was not quick she would bump into it. She plunged the left oar into the water, hoping to turn the boat, but the oar went in flat and she nearly fell over backwards. At the same moment a voice sounded almost in her ear – a high, childish voice with a tremble of laughter in it.

"Quick! Throw me the rope!"

Chapter Nine

A GIRL AND A BOAT

ANNA THREW THE rope, felt the jerk as it tightened, and the boat was drawn in until it bumped gently against the wall.

She looked up. Standing above her, at the top of what she now saw was a flight of steps cut into the wall, was a girl. The same girl as she had seen before. She was wearing a long, flimsy dress, and her fair hair fell in strands over her shoulders as she bent forward, peering down into the boat.

"Are you all right?" she whispered.

"Yes," said Anna, in her ordinary voice.

"Ssh!" The girl lifted a finger to her lips. "Don't let anyone hear. Can you climb out?"

Anna climbed out, the girl tied the rope to an iron ring in the wall, and they stood together at the top of the steps, eyeing each other in the half light. This is a dream, thought Anna. I'm imagining her, so it doesn't matter if I don't say anything. And she went on staring and staring as if she were looking at a ghost. But the strange girl was looking at her in the same way.

"Are you real?" Anna whispered at last.

"Yes, are you?"

They laughed and touched each other to make sure. Yes, the girl was real, her dress was made of a light, silky stuff, and her arm, where Anna touched it, was warm and firm.

Apparently the girl, too, had accepted Anna's reality. "Your hand's sticky," she said, rubbing her own down the side of her dress. "It doesn't matter, but it is." Then she added, wonderingly, "Are you a beggar girl?"

"No," said Anna. "Why should I be?"

"You've got no shoes on. And your hair's dark and straggly, like a gipsy's. What's your name?"

"Anna."

"Are you staying in the village?"

"Yes, with Mr and Mrs Pegg."

The girl looked at her thoughtfully. In the fading light Anna could barely see her features, but she thought that her eyes were blue with straight dark lashes.

65

"I'm not allowed to play with the village children," the girl said slowly, "but you're a visitor, aren't you? Anyway, it makes no difference. They'll never know."

Anna turned away abruptly. "You needn't bother," she said.

But the girl held her back. "No, don't go! Don't be such a goose. I *want* to know you! Don't you want to know me?"

Anna hesitated. Did she want to know this strange girl? She hardly knew the answer herself. But to get things straight first, she said, "My hands are sticky because I had a bun for tea, and my hair's untidy because I haven't brushed it since this morning. I *have* got some shoes, but I left them on the beach. So now you know."

The girl laughed and pulled her down beside her on to the top step. "Let's sit here, then they won't see us if they look out. But we must talk quietly." She glanced over her shoulder, up towards the house. Anna followed her look. "They're all up there," she whispered. "That's the drawing-room where the lights are."

There was a sudden sound of a window opening just above their heads. The girl ducked down and put her hand on Anna's shoulder, making her duck down too. Silently they eased their way down a step, and sat huddled together, heads bent, the girl holding Anna's arm in a tight grip. Above them a woman's voice said, "How beautiful the marsh is at night! I could sit here for ever." The girl gave a shiver of excitement and ducked lower. They held hands, laughing silently, seeing only each other's white teeth shining in the darkness.

"Shut the window," said a man's voice from above. There was a sound of music from inside the room, then a burst of laughter and other voices. Someone called, "Marianna, come and dance!" Then the woman's voice, right overhead, said, "Yes, in a minute. By the way, where's the child?"

The girl flung her arm round Anna's waist and they held their breath. Anna did not remember ever being so close to anyone before. Then the man's voice said, "In bed, I should hope. Come on, do shut the window." There was a click as the window closed again, then silence. From the marsh came again the sound of the little grey-brown bird calling, "Pity me! Oh, pity me!" A slight breeze ruffled the water and the boat rocked gently below them. The girl let go of Anna's hand.

"Was it you they were talking about?" Anna whispered. She nodded, laughing quietly. "Then why are you in that dress? Weren't you meant to be at the party?"

"That was earlier. It's late now. I'm supposed to be in bed. You heard. Are you allowed to stay up all night?"

Anna shook her head. "No, I'll have to go soon anyway—" she paused, remembering the way she had come. "Is it your boat?" she whispered.

"Yes, of course. I left it on purpose for you. But I didn't know you couldn't row!" They chuckled together in the darkness, and Anna felt suddenly tremendously happy.

"How did you know I was here?" she asked. "Have you seen me?"

"Yes, often."

"But I thought you'd only just come!"

The girl laughed again, then clapped her hand over her mouth. She leaned towards Anna and whispered in her ear, so that it tickled. "Silly, of course not! I've been here ages."

"How long?" Anna whispered back.

"A week at least," there was a teasing note in her voice. "Ssh! Come down now and I'll row you back."

In the boat Anna said, "Have you been watching me?"

The girl nodded. "Hush! Voices carry over the water."

Anna lowered her voice. "I had a feeling you were. Sometimes I even looked round to see who it was, looking and looking like that – but you were never there."

The girl laughed softly. "I was!"

"Where?"

She leaned forward on the oars and pointed upwards. "In my window. The last one on the end."

Anna nodded slowly. "Yes, of course. I should have known. I saw you there. And I saw you last night. You were having your hair brushed."

"I saw you, too."

Anna was surprised. "But you were standing sideways, you couldn't have. You never showed—"

"No, of course I didn't— Ssh! Don't shout." – Anna had thought she was talking quietly – "Didn't you know, you're my secret? I've not told anyone about you, and I'm not going to. If I do they'll only spoil it." She leaned forward and touched Anna's knee. "Promise you won't tell about me either? Not ever?"

"Oh, no, I won't!"

Anna loved being asked. Here was someone just like herself. This was the one thing she would have chosen – to have a secret friend, a friend no-one else knew about. Someone who was real, and yet not quite real…

"What were you doing on the marsh this morning?" the girl asked dreamily.

"Picking samphire. Why, did you see me then, too?"

"Yes. I wondered if you were picking sea lavender… I love sea lavender…" Her voice had dropped so low that Anna could barely hear the last words.

The boat grated gently on the shore and she leapt out. She stood holding the bow for a moment, not speaking, unwilling to say goodbye. The girl, in her light dress against the dark background of water and marsh and reeds, looked like a small, pale ghost now. It had grown quite dark. There was silence all around except for the soft lapping of the water at Anna's feet. She looked up and saw overhead the enormous sky, peppered with stars. Yes, she thought, this is all a dream…

Then the girl said – her voice wavering a little – "You look like a ghost, standing there so still. Anna – Anna, you *are* real, aren't you?"

Anna laughed with relief, and the girl laughed too.

"Come here," she said.

Anna leaned over towards her, and the girl kissed her quickly on the cheek. "There," she said, "now I know you're real. Give me a push off quickly, before you turn into a ghost again!" Then, as Anna shoved the boat off, she called in a low voice, with what sounded like a chuckle,

"And next time I'll teach you how to row! Goodbye – don't forget your shoes!"

Anna raked about on the dark shore until she found her shoes – she would have forgotten them if the girl had not reminded her; that *proved* she was real! – and ran home trembling with excitement. She had sworn she would never get to know the family when they came, yet now she was as pleased as if she had never met anyone of her own age before.

But this girl was different. There was something almost magical about her. She realised suddenly that she did not even know her name, and slowed down to a walk for a moment, wondering confusedly why ever she had not asked. Perhaps there had not been time. She could not remember. She only knew that something wonderful seemed to have happened.

She ran up the little road towards the cottage, hearing in the distance the voices of the Bingo players coming home down the lane, laughing and talking, and calling goodnight to each other as they dropped off in ones and twos at their own gates. She raced ahead, pushed open the scullery door and saw the light burning, the kettle boiling on the stove, and the cocoa cups already laid out by Sam, and it seemed like another world…

Chapter Ten

PICKLED SAMPHIRE

AT BREAKFAST NEXT morning Anna caught Mrs Pegg looking at her with a puzzled expression. Then she remembered about the Bingo. Mrs Stubbs would have been there and she would have told her about Anna and Sandra.

Well, she was not going to think about that now. She had something far nicer to think about. She ate her breakfast quietly, smiling to herself as she remembered her adventure of last night; that strange girl, and her lovely little boat... Would she be down on the creek again tonight? She had forgotten to ask! Dismayed, she held a forkful of fried bread with a small piece of tomato balanced on top, halfway to her mouth and stared at it intently. Then she remembered that the girl said she would teach her to row next time. She smiled again, pushed the fork into her mouth, and looking up, caught Mrs Pegg's eye.

"Well, you like your breakfast, any road," said Mrs Pegg. "That's one comfort."

Anna pulled herself together. "Yes, thank you. It's very nice."

Mrs Pegg looked at her with her head on one side, thoughtfully. "Did you forget what I asked you yesterday morning?"

Anna looked up defensively. Mrs Pegg had asked her to be friendly to Sandra, and she had tried, and it had not worked. But she was not going to show she cared about that.

"Not that it matters all that much," Mrs Pegg was saying, "only Sam said to me after you'd gone, 'There,' he says, 'I could have just fancied a bit of pickled sanfer again'—"

But Sam, suddenly realising what was being said, interrupted. "No, no, leave the lass be, Susan. I can pick me own sanfer if I've a mind. Happen she'd other things to occupy her mind, hadn't you, my biddy?"

Anna looked up vaguely, only half listening. What were they talking about? Samphire? Then she remembered. She had left it behind the outhouse after meeting Sandra and had forgotten all about it. Without a word she got up and went out to fetch it, carrying it in and putting it down just inside the door.

"There now, what a surprise!" said Mrs Pegg, all smiles. "And us thinking you'd forgot! I suppose you didn't think to ask Miss Manders about the jars as well, did you, my duck?"

Anna, still standing by the door, said cautiously, "Yes, I did. She said she'd look them out later." She watched Mrs Pegg's face but saw no change in her expression, which was still one of pleased surprise. "I'll fetch them now if you like, and the vinegar," she added, trying to sound neither sullen nor ingratiating, just ordinary.

Mrs Pegg said that would be real kind, but no need to hurry as she'd plenty to do first. But Anna preferred to go straight away. She took down the string bag from its peg behind the door and went out, leaving the two of them smiling and shaking their heads at each other. She was a queer one and no mistake.

So Mrs Pegg did not know yet. Anna wondered why, then reminded herself she did not care anyway. And it was as well she had reminded herself, because the first thing Mrs Pegg said, when she came back and they were unloading the jars, was, "I'll be going up to the Corner tonight, so maybe I'll take a jar with me. Mrs Stubbs used to be partial to pickled sanfer."

"Did you see her at the Bingo?" Anna asked, as casually as she could.

74

Mrs Pegg shook her head. "No, we was at different ends of the room, but she says to me at the door after, 'Come over to mine tonight,' she says, 'there's something I want to see you about.' It'll be about them patterns her sister's brought from Lynn, I'm thinking – for the chair covers. She's been promising me this long time. I thought Mrs S didn't look too pleased neither – because I didn't go the first time she asked me, I suppose. Any road, I said I'd go tonight. So you don't mind if I'm a bit late back, do you, my duck?"

No, Anna assured her, she did not mind at all. She liked being on her own best of all; and she hardly noticed the surprised glance Mrs Pegg gave her.

It was dusk when Anna went down to the creek that evening. All afternoon Mrs Pegg had been busy, washing and pickling the samphire, and now, in her best blouse and with a jar, filled and sealed, in her hand, she had gone off to Mrs Stubbs-up-at-the-Corner. Anna had watched her go, doggedly closing her mind to the hurtfulness of the situation – poor Mrs Pegg going all unsuspecting with her little gift, only to be scolded by Mrs Stubbs about Anna's bad behaviour. Once upon a time she might have found some roundabout way of warning her beforehand, but this evening she had not even allowed herself to think about it.

She was dismayed at first to find no boat, and the water still halfway down the staithe when she got to the creek. Then she remembered that of course the tide would be nearly an hour later tonight. She hung around, sitting on the slope of the bank, and searching the shore for signs of shells or sea urchins, but finding only pieces of cork, some tarred rope, and a broken bottle top. Then it grew dark.

Depressed, she leaned up against the post where the little boat had been tied up, and told herself the girl was not coming. Already the tide had crept up the shore and was beginning to swirl sluggishly round the foot of the post. Perhaps she had imagined her after all. Perhaps the whole thing was a silly dream… And then, suddenly, there was a soft plashing of oars, the rhythmic rattle of rowlocks, and there she was, as real as real, coming nearer and nearer. Anna splashed into the water to meet her.

"I was afraid you wouldn't be here," the girl said. "Jump in quick and we'll go for a row."

"I thought you weren't coming," said Anna.

"I know. I forgot about the tide being later. I couldn't come the other way, they'd have seen me go past the windows."

She turned the boat and pulled away from the shore, upstream.

"Don't let's talk," she said. "I'll tell you why after, but first you must have a rowing lesson."

Anna took the oars, and the girl sat opposite her in the stern, leaning forward and guiding her hands. Every now and then she looked up into Anna's face, laughing silently, and took her own hands away; then Anna found she was not rowing so well, after all. But soon she was managing the oars almost alone.

She stared straight ahead of her as she rowed, her eyes wide and unblinking, straining through the darkness to take in every detail of her new friend. She saw that her straight fair hair was plaited tonight, and hung over her shoulders in two long braids which swung to and fro every time she bent forward. Under her cardigan she was again wearing a long white dress which reached almost to her feet. It would have looked strange on anyone else, but Anna accepted it almost without question. It seemed right that this girl should look like the character out of some fairy story.

At the top of the creek, where the boat could go no farther, they shipped the oars silently, and sat almost enclosed by rushes and tangled water weed, listening to the small, night sounds – a frog croaking on the bank, water dripping from the reeds, and the plop of small fish as they rose to the surface then sank again. They sat so still that each of them might have been alone. Then the girl leaned forward, and said in a half whisper, "Now I'll tell you why I said we wouldn't talk."

Chapter Eleven

THREE QUESTIONS EACH

ANNA MOVED NEARER and the girl said, still in a half whisper, "You remember I said last night that you were my secret?"

Anna nodded. "I knew just what you meant. You're mine."

"Well, that's it! Don't let's spoil it by gabbling at each other, and asking a whole lot of questions, and arguing, and perhaps end up quarrelling. Let's go on like we are."

"Yes – oh, yes!" said Anna, then hesitated. "But I don't even know your name yet."

"Marnie." The girl seemed surprised. "I thought you knew." Anna shook her head. "Listen," she went on, "there are all sorts of things I want to know about you; why you're here, and where you live, and what you do all day – things like that – and yet, in a way, I don't want to know them at all—" she broke off and laughed quickly. "No, that's wrong! I *do* want to know. But I want to find them out slowly, by myself, as we go along. Do you know what I mean?"

Yes, Anna did know. This was just how she felt.

"I'll tell you what we'll do!" said Marnie. "We'll make a pact to ask each other only one question a night, shall we? Like wishes in a fairy story."

"They're usually three," said Anna doubtfully.

"All right, we'll make it three. I'll start. Question number one – why are you here at Little Overton?"

This was fun. Anna drew a deep breath and told her about coming to stay with the Peggs instead of going back to school, because Dr Brown had said it would be good for her and she was underweight. And then, because Marnie looked so interested, she told her about not-even-trying, and Mrs Preston being worried about her future. "But it's not just that," she said. "They don't know that I know, but it's because they want to get rid of me for a bit. I'm a sort of worry to them."

"Oh, poor you! But are you sure? Sometimes it feels like that, I know, but it isn't really true."

"No, I do know. One day I'll tell you how I know, but

not tonight. Is it my turn now?" Marnie nodded. "How many brothers and sisters have you got?"

"Me?" Marnie was amazed. "None. Why should you think I had?"

"Do you mean you're the *only one*?" Anna's voice sounded quite shocked. She was disappointed. What about the boys and girls in navy blue jeans and jerseys? She had been so sure they belonged to The Marsh House too...

Marnie gave her a little push with her elbow. "What's the matter? Aren't I enough for you? – And that's not a proper question, by the way."

Anna laughed. "Yes, but I always thought you were a big family."

"Well, I suppose we are, in a way..." Marnie began counting on her fingers, "There's me, and Lily, and Ettie, and Nan, and Mother, and Father..." she hesitated – "and Pluto."

Something about the way her eyes suddenly darkened made Anna ask quickly, "Who's Pluto?"

"No, no, you're cheating! It's my turn now. Question two – are you an only, too?"

Anna considered. Did Raymond count or not? He was not really a brother or a cousin or any relation at all. "Sort of," she said at last.

"What do you mean, sort of?"

"Now you're cheating! It's my turn. Who's Pluto?"

"Our dog." Marnie looked suddenly solemn. "I'll tell

you a secret. I hate him really. He's big and black, and quite fierce sometimes. He lives in a kennel outside most of the time. Father said he'd be good company for me, but he's not. I wanted a kitten, a dear little fluffy kitten that I could nurse on my lap, but Father said Pluto'd be good for guarding the house when he's away. He wasn't so bad when he was a puppy, though even then he was too big and rough, but he's awful now. He eats *raw meat*, think of that! Don't tell anyone, but secretly I'm frightened of him." She gave a little shudder, then in an instant became merry again. "It's my turn, isn't it? What's it like, living at the Peggs'?"

Anna opened her mouth to answer and found, to her surprise, that she could not remember. Perhaps it was because she had been thinking about Marnie's answer, and wondering whether it was Pluto she sometimes heard barking in the night. What *was* it like at the Peggs'? Not one single thing could she remember. It had all gone out of her head as completely as if someone had wiped a sponge across a blackboard. Marnie, who had seemed only half real, had now become more real than the Peggs. It was odd.

She glanced across at Marnie, who seemed to have sunk into a dream of her own while waiting. She was sitting huddled in the stern with her feet up and her head bent, her face in shadow.

Anna tried again. She *must* remember about the Peggs, otherwise she would not be able to tell Marnie anything about them. She closed her eyes and saw – faintly at first, then clearly – the scullery, the kettle on the stove, and through the door, Sam's armchair with the broken springs in the corner. The Peggs and their cottage came to life again. Relieved, she opened her eyes and saw – no-one. Marnie had gone! She was alone in the boat.

She gave a little cry and sprang up, the boat rocking beneath her. At the same minute, from somewhere behind her, she heard Marnie's voice saying in a startled whisper, "Anna! What's the matter? Where are you?"

"I thought you'd gone!" said Anna. "What are you doing out there?"

Marnie was standing on the bank behind her. In her long white dress, with the reeds standing up all round her, and the moonlight shining on her pale hair, she looked more than ever like someone out of a fairy story. She came nearer, and Anna saw that she was looking quite frightened.

"Oh, you gave me a shock!" she was saying. "You shouldn't have run away. I got out to look for you. I thought you must be hiding in the reeds." She took hold of Anna's hand to steady herself and stepped back into the boat. "Don't do that again, Anna – dear." Her voice was almost pleading.

"But I didn't! I didn't do anything!"

Marnie sat down again and folded her hands in her lap. "Yes, you did," she said primly, "you played a trick on me. It wasn't fair. I asked you a question and you never answered. Instead you ran away and hid—"

"Oh, I remember now!" said Anna. "But I didn't run away. You asked me about the Peggs and what it was like there. Well, I'll tell you. It's…" her voice faltered. "It's…" She had forgotten again. It was extraordinary.

Marnie laughed gaily. "Oh, don't bother! What do I care about the Peggs? I don't even know who they are. It was a silly question anyway. Let's talk about something real. Have you got a watch on?"

"No. Why?"

"I think we ought to go back soon. It was late when we came out. They might discover I'd gone. Shall I row?"

Anna nodded, and they changed seats and pushed out from the reeds into the stream.

"You didn't have your last question," said Marnie.

"No, but I wasn't able to answer yours," said Anna, still wondering.

"Oh, that doesn't matter! I'll ask you another instead. Where do you live?"

"In London," said Anna quickly. "Twenty-five Elmwood Terrace."

Marnie nodded approvingly. "You were able to answer that one, anyway. Now you can ask your last."

Anna turned over in her mind which of many questions to ask. Should she ask Marnie about her dress? No, she had probably been to some sort of grown-up dinner party. Or about her family? No, they were only grown-ups after all. But she was still intrigued by Marnie's confession that she was frightened of her own dog. She said, at last, "Does anything else frighten you – apart from obvious things like earthquakes, I mean?"

Marnie thought seriously. "Thunderstorms, a little – if they're bad. And—" She turned and looked behind her across the fields to where the windmill stood like a solitary sentinel, dark against the sky. "That does sometimes," she said quickly, with a shiver.

"The windmill! But why?"

"Too late! You'll have to save that for next time," said Marnie, laughing again. Then she added, more seriously,

"I don't think it's a very good game after all. You seemed to ask all the wrong questions. I don't usually think of gloomy things like that old windmill. And I asked a wrong question, too. You couldn't even answer it, and frightened me by running away instead."

"I wish I knew what you meant about that," said Anna, still worrying over it. "Honestly, I never moved."

"Oh, but you did!" Marnie's eyes were round. "How can you say such a thing? I waited and waited for you to answer, and then when I looked up you just weren't there. That's why I jumped out."

"No, it was you!" said Anna indignantly.

Marnie sighed. "You think it was me, and I think it was you. Don't let's quarrel about it. Perhaps it was both of us."

"Or neither of us," said Anna, her anger slipping away. After all what did it matter? The last thing she wanted to do was quarrel with Marnie. She changed the subject quickly. "You are lucky to have a boat like this all of your own."

"I know I am. It's what I always wanted, and this year I had it for my birthday. You're the first person who's ever been in it, apart from me. Are you glad about that?" Anna was.

They drew in to the shore. "I'll drop you here," said Marnie. "Can you paddle now or is it too deep?"

Anna put a foot over the side. The water came up to just below her knee. "It's all right. For me, that is," she said, thinking of Marnie's dress.

"What do you mean, 'for you'!" said Marnie with mock indignation. "I'm as tall as you are." She laughed suddenly. "Oh, you mean my evening gown! And poor old you in your boys' clothes! Do you wish you were dressed the same as me?"

She's getting at me, thought Anna, and made no reply. But Marnie had turned the boat and was already rowing away, still chuckling.

"Goodbye!" called Anna in a small, forlorn voice – quickly before it was too late.

"Goodbye!" called Marnie, still laughing. She went on chuckling until the darkness had almost swallowed her up, then, just as she disappeared out of sight, Anna heard her call quietly, but quite distinctly, over the water.

"Silly, it's my nightie!"

Chapter Twelve

MRS PEGG BREAKS
HER TEAPOT

MRS PEGG WAS shaking the rag mat in the yard with unnecessary violence, and talking to Anna between shakes.

"I'd have thought the *least* you could do – was keep a civil *tongue* in your head – after I'd specially *asked* you to look *friendly* –" shake – shake – "I'm that *riled* with you, I—" she choked and flung the mat over the dustbin, then wiped her eyes on the corner of her apron. For one awful moment Anna thought she was crying, then realised that her own eyes were pricking. The tiny yard was full of dust.

Mrs Pegg turned on her, red in the face. "Why did you do that, lass? What come over you, for goodness sake?"

"She called *me* names first," Anna mumbled.

"Oh, she did, did she? What sort of names?" Mrs Pegg looked hopeful for an instant but Anna closed her mouth obstinately. Mrs Pegg pressed her. "Not that I'm one to listen to other's tiffs generally speaking," she said, "and what's done can't be undone, but you'd better tell me now."

"She said I looked like – just-what-I-was," said Anna, the words tumbling out all together in a sullen mumble.

"Like *what*?"

"Just-what-I-was," Anna repeated.

"Well, lordsakes, and what's wrong with that!" Mrs Pegg flung up her hands in despair and lumbered angrily indoors. From the kitchen Anna could hear Sam's voice protesting mildly that it was a small thing to get so put out about, and Mrs Pegg retorting angrily that it was all very well for him to talk, but if he'd kindly cast his mind back he might remember how she'd said all along it wouldn't do to fall out with Mrs Stubbs, not till after the fête.

"You know very well I never was one to listen to tittle-tattle and squabbles, but what with Mrs S being so put out, and her running the cake stall what I'm put down to help with—" There was a sudden crash, then Mrs Pegg's voice, shaky now, "There! Me big teapot! If that ain't the last straw—" followed by an unmistakable sob.

Anna did not wait to hear any more.

She went down to the beach, walking all the way along the dyke. There was no sign of Wuntermenny, and in any case she felt that even his company would be an interruption. She did not want to think about anyone or anything, not even Marnie. It would have been all right if only Mrs Pegg had gone on being angry, but when she had dropped that teapot… hastily Anna put the memory out of her mind. She walked hard, thinking about nothing and seeing nothing, until she came at last to the sand dunes.

Here was the one place where she could be sure of meeting no-one. Even if anyone should happen to be wandering along the beach, she could see them while they were still no more than a speck in the distance, and lie low until they had passed. Already she had spent many afternoons here, lying in a sandy hollow, hearing only the wind rustling the tops of the grasses, the distant crying of the gulls, and the soft soughing of the sea. It was like being at the very edge of the world. Sometimes the gulls came nearer, screaming noisily as they quarrelled over small fish in the pools, and sometimes they cried mournfully far away along the beach. Then Anna felt like crying too – not actually, but quietly – inside. They made a sad, and beautiful, and long-ago sound that seemed to remind her of something lovely she had once known – and lost, and never found again. But she did not know what it was.

So, this morning, she spent several hours in the sand dunes, not thinking about Mrs Pegg, and not thinking about Sandra or Mrs Stubbs, and only thinking about Marnie when she had emptied her mind of everything else. And it was then that she realised the tide would not be high until even later that night. It would be after eleven o'clock. How was she going to see Marnie?

Walking home again at dinner-time, she thought of the obvious answer. If Marnie could go out in a nightdress, so could she! She would go to bed early tonight, before the Peggs, and slip out later. And this afternoon, when the tide was out, she would pick a bunch of sea lavender for Marnie.

A letter from Mrs Preston was waiting for her at the cottage when she got back. It told her all sorts of news about people she did not know, whom she supposed must be neighbours at home. But when she tried to visualise home it seemed so unreal and far away that she found it difficult to imagine Mrs Preston still living there. A postscript at the bottom said, *Do write again soon. You didn't tell us much except that you went to the beach. And you didn't say anything about the smell either, dear. Can you describe it?*

Anna was surprised. The smell... what smell? Or perhaps the word was "shell"? She examined it closely and saw that it was not. A stamped addressed card had been included this time so she decided to reply at once before she forgot again, and while Mrs Pegg laid the table around her, she wrote, "The beach doesn't smell." This was untrue, of course. The beach had a wonderful smell, but "Can you describe it?" reminded Anna of Miss Davison's English exercises at school, and her resistance was aroused. In any case, how could you describe the smell of the beach? It just smelled of the sea, or seaweed – though occasionally, if the wind were in the wrong direction, and nature had done her worst – of a dead seal. But who wanted to hear about the smell of a dead seal on a postcard? Instead, she gave an accurate account of the weather and (since this was uppermost in her mind) the state of the tides during the last few days.

After dinner she went out again, waited until the tide was low enough, then paddled across to the marsh to pick her sea lavender.

Mrs Pegg, seeing Anna's postcard still on the mantelpiece, stamped and ready for posting, clicked her tongue. Really, the child would forget her head one of these days! She had specially reminded her to post it when she went out. She picked it up and looked at it curiously, with her eyes screwed up, turning it in all directions.

"Well, I don't know!" she said. "I never were no scholar, but – here, you read that." She handed it to Sam. "What does that say?"

Sam read aloud, laboriously, "The – beach – doesn't – smell."

"There!" said Mrs Pegg triumphantly. "That's what I thought it said!"

"Well, that don't smell, do it?"

"No. And the moon ain't blue. And cows don't dance. And some folks ain't got the sense they was born with. You, for one, Sam Pegg. Don't it strike you that's a queer way for a child to start a letter?"

"Oh, ah! Happen she'd other things on her mind," said Sam.

"Happen she had," said Mrs Pegg, shaking her head in a vaguely bewildered way. "Happen she always has, if you ask me." Then she went out, posted the card, and forgot about it.

That evening, as soon as the Peggs had settled down to their evening television, Anna fetched a book and sat reading near them on a low stool. After a while she began yawning and let the book slip sideways. When she had sat there long enough for her boredom with the book and her weariness with the programme to be noticed by the Peggs – or so she hoped – she rose and yawned again. Then, to the accompaniment of massed brass bands from an agricultural hall somewhere in East Anglia, she tiptoed hurriedly, with ostentatious quietness, towards the stairs.

Once in her own room, she undressed and put on her nightdress. Then she pulled on her shorts, tucking the nightdress inside, and put on her jersey on top. Now she was ready. She waited until she judged the tide would be well on the way up, then picking up the bunch of sea lavender, she opened her door and listened. Then, still under cover of the noise from the television, she crept downstairs and slipped out through the scullery door.

The Peggs, sitting like two ancient monuments in the flickering blue light, had their backs towards her and never even turned round.

Chapter Thirteen

THE BEGGAR GIRL

THE BOAT WAS waiting. Anna stepped in and cast off the rope. In a moment, almost before she had time to dip the oars, she was drifting steadily along in the direction of The Marsh House. She scarcely needed to row; the boat seemed to know its own way.

She was nearly opposite the house when she was startled to see there were lights in all the windows. What could it mean? And the sound of music was coming over the water! She rested on the oars and held her breath. This was what she had dreamed of – a party going on in the old house! As the little boat drifted slowly past, she saw, through the windows, the great staircase ablaze with light, and the bright colours of the ladies' dresses moving about inside. And in the dark water, just as she had imagined it, she saw it all reflected, the lights spearing down in trembling points almost to the very edge of the boat.

Then she had passed the house. Turning, she saw, in the darkness behind her, a small white figure standing at the top of the projecting wall. It was Marnie, waiting for her.

She threw the rope and Marnie caught it. Once more she was pulled gently in, alongside the steps. She clambered out and Marnie caught hold of her hand.

"Oh, I'm so glad you've come!" she whispered. "Did you hear the music?"

"Yes, and I saw the lights. It looked so lovely from the water I thought I must be dreaming it!"

"They're having a party," Marnie whispered. "I was so hoping I'd see you! I've run out to look for you over and over again."

"I thought I mightn't be able to come tonight, it's so late," said Anna. "But look…" she pulled her nightdress out from under her shorts, "I've done the same as you. I've got ready for bed first!" Then she saw that Marnie was wearing a real white party dress, with a full skirt and a ribbon sash.

"I had to," Marnie said apologetically. "It's a grown-up party, really, but I had to be there. One or two of them

95

are quite young – but *years* older than us." She squeezed Anna's hand and snuggled up to her. "I'm so glad you're here. I wish you could come in, too…" she hesitated, looking at her thoughtfully, then suddenly she laughed. "I know! You *shall* come in. Nobody will know who you are."

"But I can't," Anna protested, "not in a nightie and sandshoes." She glanced down and saw that her nightdress was now streaked with mud. "I can't," she repeated sadly. "Anyway, I'm all muddy."

"Yes, you can! The muddier the better. I've an idea. You only want a shawl over your head and you'll look like a beggar girl." Then she saw the bunch of sea lavender in Anna's hands. "Oh, you darling, you've brought me some sea lavender! That's just what we need. You're a beggar girl, and you've come to sell sea lavender to the ladies and gentlemen – for luck. *Will* you? Wait, and I'll fetch you a shawl!" Without waiting for an answer she ran in by a side door, leaving Anna standing alone on the wall.

Anna was not frightened. She was hardly nervous. She had no very clear idea what was going to happen and, oddly enough, it never entered her head that she had any choice in the matter. She felt, as she always did with Marnie, that what ever they did was the only thing they could have done. It had all been decided already. Anna had only to wait and see what happened. So she waited now, standing in sandshoes, and a muddy nightdress over a pair of cotton shorts, listening to the sounds of music coming from the house behind her and beginning to feel quietly excited.

Marnie came running back with an old brown shawl in her hand.

"Here you are," she cried, "the very thing!" and she flung it over Anna's head, arranging it over the back of her hair and crossing the ends over her chest. Then she stood back and looked at her critically. "You look fine, but your nightie's a tiny bit too long. It ought to come just below your knees." She tucked it up round the top of Anna's shorts and they giggled together.

"Can I really?"

"Yes, of course. Oh, isn't this fun! Now your shoes –"

Marnie bent down and pushed a sprig of sea lavender into the eyelet hole of each shoe, covering the laces, then she tucked another into Anna's hair, just over one ear.

"There – now you look *exactly* right!" she said, standing back to admire her. It was as if she had already seen a picture of the person Anna was to be, and was copying it in every detail. "Now listen to me. Don't say anything but just do what I tell you. I'll go in first and warn them. You stay just inside.

"Now," she said, and they stepped in through the side door.

"Wait," and she ran down the dark passage and flung open the door at the far end. At once there was a sudden blaze of light and colour. Men and women in dark uniforms and shining dresses were moving to and fro. Anna saw the sparkle of jewellery, the gleam of gold braid, light shining on wineglasses, on silver bowls of red and cream roses, and a background of crimson curtains. The passage was suddenly filled with the sound of voices and laughter and music.

She saw Marnie, her white sash flying, running up to a tall man in uniform, who was standing in the centre of a group, with a wineglass in his hand, and pull at the gold braid on his sleeve. He bent down and she whispered something in his ear. For a moment he looked puzzled, then, laughing, he straightened his back and clapped his hands.

"Listen, everybody!" he said. "Marnie tells me we have a visitor. There is a gipsy girl at the door selling sea lavender. Who would like to buy some sea lavender for luck?" He moved towards the door, laughing indulgently, and peered down the passage, but Marnie ran ahead of him and seizing Anna by the hand, pulled her into the room.

The lights were so bright and there were so many people that Anna was quite dazzled. She stood just inside the door, her dark hair hanging in wispy curls over her face, the brown shawl clutched together in one hand and the bunch of sea lavender in the other.

"Come," said the man kindly, "don't be frightened.

What is your name?"

Anna opened her mouth to speak but no sound came out. She seemed to have been struck dumb, and she found that she had even forgotten her own name! She stared at the man, slowly shaking her head from side to side. Other people crowded round and asked her questions. Where had she come from? Who was she? How had she come? But to all of them Anna could only reply by shaking her head from side to side in the same dazed way.

"She looks like a little witch!" exclaimed a young man. "Why don't you speak, little witch? Who are you? Did you fly in on a broomstick?" They all laughed. A lady in a blue dress leaned over her. Anna saw her long, glittering necklace swinging only a few inches in front of her eyes.

"Poor child," she said, "she is dumb. Don't torment her with questions." And to Anna, gently, in a voice that was ever so slightly mocking, "Don't mind them. May I have some of your sea lavender?"

Anna nodded gravely, and handed her the bunch.

"Oh, no, that is too much!" The lady threw up her hands in exaggerated dismay, "I only want a spray for luck. And you must be paid. Of course, you must be paid!" She looked round, spreading out her hands appealingly. "Who will pay for my flowers?"

Immediately four or five young men dashed up with silver coins and tried to press them on Anna. But Anna shook her head, refusing to accept them.

"No, *I* will pay," said the tall man with the gold braid on his sleeves, and brushing them aside, he took a bunch of crimson roses from one of the silver bowls, and laid them in Anna's lap. Again Anna shook her head, but the man had already turned away. Anna picked out one rose and laid the rest aside on a table. She tucked the rose in the knot of her shawl. It smelled very sweet.

The lady in the blue dress was separating the sea lavender into small bunches and calling to the others to come and take one each, for luck. She took a sprig for herself and put it in her hair, then she put others in the men's buttonholes, in the women's dresses, insisting that everyone should wear them.

Anna watched, unnoticed. The grown-ups seemed to have forgotten her. They were laughing a lot, mocking each other, and now they seemed to be playing some sort of game. Someone threw the remaining sprays high into the air and they ran to catch them. They began tossing them to each other across the room, and Anna saw a sprinkling of grey dust fall from the dry flowers on to the floor.

A big man with pink cheeks and white hair came up to her and offered her a glass of red wine.

"Your health, my little lavender girl!" he said, and bowed low; so low that Anna could see only the top of his pink head with the curly white hair growing round it like a crown.

She took the glass and smiled, and he moved away. She wondered whether she should drink it, and looked around for Marnie, but she had disappeared.

The music struck up again and they started dancing. Anna saw Marnie again. She was on the far side of the room, waltzing with a tall, fair-haired boy of about sixteen. Anna was surprised to see how well she could dance, although she was so young. In this strange, foreign world even Marnie seemed to have become a stranger.

Someone had put a chair for Anna, and the dancers swept by, the women's light dresses brushing against her legs. She took a sip of the wine. It tasted strong and sweet. She had never tasted wine before and was not sure if she liked it. She took another sip. The bright dresses swirled past her. The music made her feel light-headed. There was a strange exciting smell on the air – the smell of wine, cigar smoke, and perfume, mingling with the scent of the roses. She took another sip from the glass and began to feel drowsy. The big man with pink cheeks and curly white hair appeared beside her with another glass of wine and held it out to her, saying something. The music drowned his words, but the lady in blue suddenly darted between them and seized the glass from his hand, saying, "No, no. She is only a child. Come and dance with me," and swept him away again. Anna could hear her laughter as she spun him around, her long necklace flying out behind her, and her blue skirts floating... floating... The bright colours merged into one another, the music rose and fell, and Anna felt herself drifting away into sleep...

Chapter Fourteen

AFTER THE PARTY

"OUGHT YOU TO go now, do you think? Will they be missing you?"

Anna had no idea how much later it was that Marnie had come up behind her and was whispering in her ear. She shook herself awake and sat up, rubbing her eyes. The music was fainter now and seemed to be coming from farther away. She saw that the guests had moved through into another room, beyond the crimson curtains. For the moment she and Marnie were alone.

"Ought I? What time is it?"

"I don't know, but I think the tide's on the turn. If you come now I'll take you back in the boat, but we'd better not wait too long. Once the tide's out you'll have to walk along the staithe in the slippery mud, it's better to go now. Come now while no-one's looking."

"All right." Anna rose to her feet and stumbled out of the room, following Marnie along the passage to the side door. Outside it was cool and quiet. There was a sound of water lapping, and a fresh salt smell. Beyond the marsh she could hear the soughing of the sea, and distant waves breaking on the beach.

As they reached the top of the steps they heard a door opening behind them and looked back. The tall, fair-haired boy was standing silhouetted against a strip of light in the doorway, looking this way and that, as if searching for someone. Marnie seized her hand and they ducked down. "Ssh! Don't let him see you."

The door closed again. They stepped down into the boat and pushed off silently. Marnie laughed quietly. "He's a nuisance – always following me about to make sure I don't get into mischief. I'm glad he didn't see us."

"Why? – Don't you like him?" Anna had thought he looked a nice boy, but if Marnie said not she was ready to agree.

Marnie said impatiently, "Oh, yes, he's all right, but he always makes it his business to look after me, and sometimes it's a bore. Look, here we are. Can you step out here, then I needn't pull the boat ashore."

Anna stepped out, holding her shoes in her hand, still clutching the shawl round her neck.

"Goodbye, beggar girl!" said Marnie, laughing.

"Oh, I forgot!" Anna untied the knot of the shawl. Something small and dark dropped into the water. "Oh, my rose!" she cried. But it was too late; already it was beyond her reach, floating away into the darkness.

Marnie laughed at her dismay. "It was only a rose," she said. "There are plenty more."

Anna dropped the shawl into the boat. "Goodbye," she said. "It was lovely – I never even *imagined*..." she stopped suddenly, remembering. "Tomorrow – the tide – it will be so late..."

"Yes, oh bother!" Marnie considered, nodding her head thoughtfully up and down. "Never mind. I'll see you – somewhere, some time, I can't promise where or when. But keep looking out for me – *please*—" She turned sharply as a dog began barking loudly from somewhere beyond The Marsh House – "That'll be Pluto. That means some of them are leaving already. I must go." She took hold of the oars and repeated, "Keep looking out for me. And remember, you promise not to tell – ever?"

"Oh, yes, I promise!"

Already the boat was moving away. Anna sat down by the edge of the water, listening to the quiet plip-plop of the oars fading into the distance, until there was only the soft wash of ripples on the shore.

What a wonderful evening it had been! She was sure she would never be able to sleep tonight. It seemed absurd to go back to the cottage and lie tossing and turning on her bed with all those magical sights and sounds still going on in her head. The night air seemed full of them still – the tinkle of the piano, the bursts of laughter, glowing colours and the sparkle of jewels, Marnie's voice, the flick of her white sash as she ran ahead down the dark passage…

But even as she sat there, dreaming about it, the music faded, the merry grown-ups in their gold-braided uniforms and bright dresses drifted away like ghosts… She laid her head on her knee. A wandering night breeze lifted her hair and cooled her hot cheeks.

"Hello – hello! What have we got here?"

Anna woke with a jump to find three large figures standing over her, talking loudly.

"Well, bless my soul if it ain't the little-old-girl from up at Peggs'!"

"That's a strange place for a little lass to be sitting in the middle of the night!"

She jumped to her feet quickly.

"There now, love, it's only us – Mr and Mrs Beales from up at The Cobbles. Come you back home along of us; we go right by yours. I should think Mrs Pegg'll be wondering where you've got to, won't she?" A large warm

arm, round and solid as a bolster, went round Anna's shoulders and she found herself being led up the road between the three of them. "Are you all right, love?" Mrs Beales sounded concerned. "Mercy me, your poor little old feet! Where's your shoes, then?"

"I'm carrying them, thank you," said Anna stiffly. "I like walking with bare feet. I'm only hobbling because I've been sitting still. Is it – is it very late?"

"Quite late enough, I'm thinking," said Mrs Beales, adding over Anna's head to her friend, "I can't think what Susan Pegg's dreaming of – at this time of night! My Sharon's been in bed these last four or five hours. But there, Susan Pegg don't know a thing about children – never had none of her own, you see." She bent down to Anna and shouted consolingly, "I'll tell you what, love, if ever you feels lonely of an evening you could always come up to ours and have a look at telly. Young Sandra-up-at-the-Corner often do, when her mum's out at committees and such. Would you like that, now?"

Anna thanked her and thought she would hate it, but did not say so.

Mrs Pegg was at the cottage door, putting out the milk bottles. She looked astonished when she saw Anna.

"Lordsakes, I thought you was in bed this long while!" she exclaimed. "And Mary Beales – and Ethel – and Mr Beales! Good evening all. And what's to do with our Anna for goodness sake?"

107

"Down by the creek she was, fast asleep, as true as we're standing here – warn't she, Ethel? We'd been up to Whist Drive and popped in to Alice on the way back, and come round home by way of the staithe for a breath of air, and there she was as—"

Mrs Pegg bent over Anna. "Run you on in, love, and get yourself a cup of milk. After twelve it is. Telly's been over this long while. That's late for a little maid to be out, that is."

Anna ran in and fetched herself a mug of milk from the pantry. She could still hear their voices murmuring in the open doorway in tones of low, shocked surprise: "Fast asleep she was. As true as I'm standing here. Setting right down by the water she was – bare feet and all. Do you think she's all right? That's a strange way for a child to be—"

But Anna did not mind. They could talk about her as much as they liked for all she cared. She had other friends now.

Still in a dream she ran up the dark, narrow staircase and lifted the latch of her own room. In the dark she went to put her shoes together under the chair, and found that she had only one after all. She must have dropped the other on the way home. Never mind... She took off her jersey and shorts and tumbled into bed, thinking she would go and look for it tomorrow – early in the morning before the others were up. The tide would be out again by then...

She fell asleep with the soughing of the sea still in her ears. And when, a little later, the moon came up over the edge of the low sill, it sent a beam of light straight across the floor to where one sandshoe lay, with a sprig of sea lavender still stuck in its eyelet hole.

Chapter Fifteen

"LOOK OUT FOR ME AGAIN!"

ANNA DID FIND her other shoe, though not till late next day. She woke late after all, spent the day wandering about the beach, and came back in the evening to find her shoe perched on top of the post where Marnie's boat had been tied up. There was no note with it, nothing to show who had found it. Possibly Marnie herself had put it there. There was no knowing.

Nothing had been said at the cottage about Anna staying out so late, and having to be brought home by the Beales.

All that day, and the next, she went about quietly, steeling herself against reproaches and scoldings that never came. And gradually she thought she understood why. Mrs Pegg knew now that Anna was not worth bothering about. And this was her way of dealing with it – by saying nothing at all. She was tired of Anna. She had tried to be kind to her and it had not worked. Now she was "letting her get on with it".

This was not so, but Anna was not to know. At home things had a way of lingering on. They were not necessarily referred to, but you could feel them in the air. Anna would be reminded of them by Mrs Preston's anxious, watchful glances, by her over-careful avoidance of the actual subject. So now, when Mrs Pegg – busily turning out the front room, preparatory to making the new covers – merely said, "Run along now, lass. I'm that busy," Anna was doubly suspicious. There were no worried glances, no conscientious attempts to talk lightly about other things. Mrs Pegg appeared entirely unconcerned. This, thought Anna, could only mean that she had abandoned her, because she was too bad to be worth bothering about.

So, unobtrusively, she made herself even scarcer, finding less to say, and staying out of doors even longer. More than ever now was she "no trouble at all".

It was all the better, she told herself as she wandered along the staithe. If the Peggs had given up bothering about her, it made it all the easier for her to give up bothering about them.

She had not seen Marnie since the party three nights ago, and The Marsh House had been silent. She glanced towards it now and saw that it seemed dark and asleep. The suspicion entered her mind suddenly that perhaps the family had gone away without her knowing. Dismayed, she turned towards an old hulk that lay permanently on its side above the water line. Here she could lie for hours, unseen by anyone. She climbed up and dropped down inside – and there was Marnie!

She was lying on her back in the bottom, wearing a blue linen smock and white socks, and sandals, and with her hands under her head was staring straight up into Anna's astonished face. "Hello," she said, laughing quietly.

"Marnie! I thought you'd gone away."

"Silly, I live here."

"But I never see you."

"Goose, you're seeing me now." Anna laughed, but Marnie put a hand lightly over her mouth. "Hush! They'll hear and come and find us."

They talked in low voices lying huddled in the bottom of the boat.

"I've been so lonely," said Anna, surprised to hear herself saying it – it was so rare for her to confide in anyone.

"Poor you. But so have I."

"You! What, with a whole houseful of jolly people?"

Marnie turned to look at her with surprised blue eyes.

"Oh, you mean the people at the party? They've gone, ages ago – two days at least. I'm all on my own now."

"Not all alone in that big house?"

"Oh, well – apart from the others, I mean, but I don't count them. Nan's not much use. She's not even much good at looking after me. She spends nearly all her time in the kitchen, drinking tea and telling fortunes in the tea leaves – not that *I* mind."

"Who's Nan? I thought you hadn't got any sisters."

Marnie laughed delightedly. "Sisters? Of course not. Nan's my nurse."

"Nurse! Are you ill, then? Is that why you're here? What's the matter with you?" In her concern, Anna asked the questions quickly, one after the other. She was amazed when Marnie turned on her, suddenly furious.

"What do you mean, what's the matter with me, you saucy girl?"

Anna drew back, startled. "Don't get huffy. It's not your fault if you're ill. I've been ill too – only you said you had a nurse to look after you."

Marnie laughed again. "Oh, you funny goose! I didn't mean a sick nurse – why should you think I meant that? – I meant my own nurse, to look after my clothes, brush my hair, take me for walks – that sort of thing. Not that she ever does take me for walks, hardly ever anyway, but *I* don't mind."

Anna was relieved. Marnie was odd, the way she was angry one minute and laughing the next, but at least she was still friendly. And she understood now. This strange girl must be very rich; the sort of girl you read about in books but never met in real life. She felt a pang of envy, remembering how she had first seen her from the boat, having her hair brushed in the upper window. Fancy having a nurse to look after your clothes!

Marnie, as if she had read her thoughts, looked curiously at Anna's shorts.

"Why do you always wear those?"

"Why not?" said Anna. "They're more comfortable." She glanced in turn at Marnie's smock, which secretly she thought looked more like a best dress. "Why don't you?"

"I wouldn't be allowed." Marnie looked regretful for a moment, then tossed her head. "Anyway, it doesn't look right." She sprang up suddenly. "Bother! That was the bell, I must go."

"I didn't hear anything."

Marnie laughed as if she didn't believe her. "You didn't *want* to hear," she said. "Anyone can hear our dinner bell halfway down the creek." She looked down at Anna, still lying on her elbow in the bottom of the hulk. "I wish I didn't have to go. Look out for me again!" she whispered quickly. Then she scrambled over the side and was gone.

Anna did look out for her. Every day she looked in the old hulk, and along the staithe, and up at the windows of The Marsh House. She was nowhere to be seen. Once she thought she saw a splash of blue in the grass along the dyke, and ran, feeling sure it was Marnie's blue smock, but when she drew near she found it was only a piece of coloured wrapping paper caught up in a small bush, and blowing in the wind. Another time, thinking it was her in the distance on the marsh, she hurried, slithering, and jumping over the pools, only to find a small boy in a blue plastic mackintosh, damming a stream with lumps of mud. His mother sat nearby reading a magazine, and Anna turned and ran before she should look up and speak to her.

Then one day she went down to the beach in Wuntermenny's boat, and while he was away along the shore collecting driftwood, she went down to the water's edge and, stooping, began searching for sea urchins along the tide line. And suddenly there was Marnie beside her.

She jumped and let out a squeak of surprise. "Where – where ever did you spring from?"

"Up there." Marnie laughed, hopping about beside her on the hard wet sand with bare feet. "I've been up in the sandhills. I was there when you first came, but I didn't want to meet *him*," she jerked her head sideways towards the distant Wuntermenny. "Isn't it fun! I left my socks and shoes up there in a hollow. It's *glorious* having bare feet, isn't it?" She stopped and peered into Anna's face. "You've been crying."

"I haven't."

"Yes, you have, but it doesn't matter. What have you been doing?"

"Only looking for sea urchins, but they're all broken." Anna crumpled the one she had been holding and flung it into the sea. "That was the best, but that was broken too."

"You are a funny girl," said Marnie, "I don't believe you've been crying about the sea urchins being broken. It's something else. Tell me what."

Anna shook her head. "I don't know, really. Truly."

"Is it what you said the other night, about them wanting to get rid of you at home? You said you knew why, but it was a sort of secret."

Anna hesitated. Was it? She hardly knew. Anyway this was the wrong minute for talking. Already she could see that Wuntermenny was preparing to come back. "Look," she said, pointing along the shore, "he's tying up the wood into a bundle. In a minute he'll start dragging it back on the rope. We can't talk now."

"Bother, oh bother!" Marnie looked annoyed. "I thought we had the beach to ourselves." She seized Anna's hand and began running up towards the sandhills, pulling her along with her. "Meet me somewhere tomorrow," she said quickly. "Can you get out early in the morning?"

"Oh, yes! I was going to go mushrooming."

"Good. Where will you be?"

"Along the marsh, towards the windmill." Marnie's face clouded for an instant. "Sam said that was the best placc. I thought I'd go down the other dyke."

"Oh, all right. Stay on the dyke, then, till I come. Then I'll be sure to see you. I'll come over the fields. Run now, before he comes back!"

Marnie danced up the slope, waved her hand and disappeared into the sandhills. And Anna ran down to the water's edge again, laughing secretly to herself as Wuntermenny came trudging up with the rope over his shoulder and his eyes bent on the ground. He had never even seen Marnie.

Chapter Sixteen

MUSHROOMS AND SECRETS

ANNA WOKE EARLY next day, happier than she had been for a long while, and crept out of the house before even Mrs Pegg was stirring. Today she was going mushrooming with Marnie!

She ran along the coast road, her hair streaming in the wind, past the crossroads and the farm where the cows were already being milked. It was a splendid, breathtaking morning, with brilliant sunshine and a strong warm wind blowing from the south west, fresh and sweet, with no sting in it – only a smell of sea and grass and marsh.

She came to a row of cottages with their curtains still pulled, and stopped for a moment to get her breath. As she leaned over the low fence, looking at the clumps of dahlias and gladioli swaying in the cottage garden, the wind dropped suddenly and she heard the rich, low chiming of a clock striking seven inside the house. It was such a cosy, indoor sound – reminding her of Sunday afternoons, boiled eggs for tea, and honey with hot scones – that for a moment she almost forgot where she was. Then the wind blew up again, warm and jolly and boisterous, and she ran on again, glad not to be shut up in that stuffy cottage.

On the farther dyke – another long, grassy bank that stretched as far as the sea – she stopped and looked around for Marnie. But there was no sign of her yet.

She walked along the dyke, looking around as she went, amazed how far she could now see over the flat countryside. To her right, cows were grazing in a distant field, looking like tiny wooden models painted in splodges of brown and white, and black and white. Away to her left the windmill, looking like a brightly painted toy, was shining in the early morning sun. And in front of her lay the marsh, shimmering in a heat haze, with the blue line of the sea beyond it.

But nowhere could she see Marnie.

She was disappointed. She sat down among the grasses and wild flowers that covered the dyke, and fixed her eyes on the distant fields. She knew that as soon as she saw the tiny blob of blue that would be Marnie's smock moving across the fields, everything would be all right. It would take at least ten minutes, running, for her to reach the place where Anna sat, but it would be all right. Marnie would have kept her promise.

She heard a rustle in the grass beside her, and a tiny noise that might have been a chuckle. She looked down and saw Marnie's face laughing up at her from the bank.

"You do look a solemn goose, staring like that. What are you looking for, mushrooms in the sky?"

"Goodness!" Anna was amazed. "However did you get here? You're almost magic!" She saw then that Marnie must have been lying in the grass on the other side of the dyke, and had merely pushed her way up silently on her stomach, lying low to surprise her. But it did seem very odd the way Marnie always appeared right beside her when she least expected it.

"Come on, slow coach, mushrooms!" Marnie seized her hand and together they ran down into the field, their hair blowing out behind them, their ears deafened by the noise of the wind. It buffeted them this way and that, almost knocking them over, like some big playful animal. Marnie knew all the best places for mushrooms, and in a while they had picked enough to fill the two paper bags Anna had brought with her.

They flung themselves down on the bank again, laughing.

"How on earth did you know exactly where to go each

time?" Anna asked. "I couldn't even see those little button ones till we were right on top of them."

"Well, I ought to know the best places by now," said Marnie. "I've been here long enough."

"You are lucky." Anna was envious. "How long?"

"Every summer of my life – as long as I can remember."

Anna, watching her, saw that her eyes were the same colour as the sea, and her hair, blowing across her face, was pale yellow, like the dry grasses on the dyke, only lighter. She thought she was the prettiest girl she had ever seen, and hated her own dark hair and sunburnt skin. I look like a witch compared with her, she thought, hating herself.

"What are you looking so gloomy about, all of a sudden?" said Marnie. She slid down the side of the bank into a hollow. "Come down here, out of the wind."

They lay, side by side, sucking the ends of grasses, while the wind roared by over their heads, scarcely stirring their hair. In the sudden quiet, Anna murmured, "You are lucky. I wish I was you."

"Why?"

Anna wanted to say, because you're pretty and rich and nice, and you've got everything I haven't, but she was suddenly tongue-tied. It would have sounded so silly. She chewed the end of her grass gloomily and said nothing.

"Tell me now who wanted to get rid of you, and why," said Marnie. "Don't your parents love you?"

Anna shook her head. "I haven't any parents. I'm – well,

sort of adopted. I live with Mr and Mrs Preston. They're called Uncle and Auntie, but they're not really."

"Oh, poor you! And are they cruel to you?" Marnie sounded almost as if she hoped they were.

"No, they're very kind to me," said Anna. "At least, she is. I don't see him very much, he's always busy, but I think he's kind too. He's quite nice."

"But what happened to your real parents?"

"My father went away – I don't know where – and my mother married someone else," Anna's voice was flat and monotonous – "and then they went away on a holiday – and I was staying with my granny – and they got killed in a car accident."

"Oh, *poor* you!" Marnie was suddenly sympathetic. "How dreadful for you. Did you go into mourning? Did you mind terribly?"

"No, I didn't mind at all. I don't even remember it. I told you, I was living with my granny…"

"Go on."

"Well, then she died," said Anna flatly.

"Oh, but why?"

Anna shrugged and pulled up another long grass, biting it between her teeth. "How should I know? She went away to some place because she said she wasn't very well, and she promised to come back soon, but she didn't. She died instead, at least that's what Miss Hannay said."

"Who's Miss Hannay?"

"A lady who comes to see me sometimes. At least, she comes to see Mrs Preston and talk about me. It's her job, you see, to go and see children who're sort of adopted like I am. She has to see me, too, and she asks about school and things. She's quite nice, but I never know what to say to her. I did ask her once about Granny – because I sort of remembered her – and she said she'd died." She paused, then added defiantly, "So what! Who cares?"

Marnie looked shocked. "But didn't you love her?"

Anna was silent for a moment, frowning at the ground. Then she blurted out sullenly, "No, I hate her. And I hate my mother. I hate them all. That's the thing…"

Marnie looked at her with puzzled eyes. "But your mother couldn't *help* being killed," she said.

Anna looked surly. "She left me before she was killed," she said defensively, "to go away on a holiday."

"And your granny couldn't help dying," said Marnie, still being reasonable.

"She left me, too," Anna insisted. "She went away. And she promised to come back and she didn't." She gave a dry little sob, then said angrily, "I hate her for leaving me all alone, and not staying to look after me. It wasn't *fair* of her to leave me – I'll never forgive her. I hate her."

Marnie said, trying to comfort her, "In a way I think you're lucky to be sort of adopted. I've often thought, secretly, that I'm adopted – don't tell, will you? – and in a way I wish I was. That would prove how *terribly* kind my mother and father are, to have adopted me when I was a poor little orphan baby with no-one to look after me."

It was Anna's turn to be surprised. "I should have thought anyone would rather have their own mother and father – if they knew them," she said, turning over another secret trouble in her mind. She looked at Marnie thoughtfully. "If I tell you a deep secret will you promise never to tell?"

"Of course! We're telling secrets all the time, aren't we? I wouldn't *dream* of telling."

"Well, it's about Mr and Mrs Preston. I told you they're kind to me, and they are, but I thought they looked after me and everything because they – well, because I was like their own child, but I found out a little while ago—" she lowered her voice almost to a whisper, "*they're paid to do it.*"

"Oh, no!" Marnie's eyes grew wide. "Are you sure? How do you know?"

"I found a letter, it was in the sideboard drawer. It was a printed letter and it was something about how the council was going to increase the allowance for me, and there was a cheque inside as well."

"Oh!" Marnie breathed. "What ever did you do?"

"When she came home I tried to ask her about it. I couldn't say I'd read the letter, at least I didn't want to. Anyway I wanted to ask her first. So I said didn't it cost an awful lot to feed me, and hadn't my new winter coat cost a lot, and things like that. And all she said was that they *liked* to do it and I wasn't to worry, and if it was because

I'd heard her saying they were hard up I wasn't to take it seriously. Everyone said they were hard up and it didn't mean anything."

She paused for breath, then went on quickly, "So I kept on asking questions about money and how much things cost, and things like that. I tried and tried. I gave her every chance I could to tell me. But she wouldn't. She just kept on saying she loved me and I wasn't to worry. Then afterwards – when I went to look – the letter had gone. She'd hidden it. So then I knew it was true."

Marnie was thinking seriously. "Does that mean she doesn't love you, though?"

"I think in a way she does, sort of," said Anna, trying to be fair. "But you can see the difference, can't you? How would you like to have someone *paid* to love you? Anyway, after that, I think she guessed that I knew. She kept looking at me as if she was worried, and wanting to know why I was always asking questions about money. And she kept trying to do things to please me. But it wasn't the same then – it couldn't be."

Marnie had an idea. "Why don't you ask Miss Hannay?"

"Oh, no!" Anna looked shocked. "That would be mean. Anyway I couldn't talk to her about it, I hardly know her. She knows all about me, but I don't know anything about her, not really. It would have been mean to ask her behind their backs. Anyway I knew already. I didn't need her to tell me what I'd found out for myself. But—" her voice broke suddenly and a tear trickled down the side of her nose, "I did so wish she'd told me herself. I gave her such a lot of chances."

Marnie moved nearer and touched her hair. "Dear Anna, *I* love you more than any girl I've ever known." She wiped the tear away and said, suddenly merry again, "There! Does that make you feel better?"

Anna smiled. Yes, she did feel better. It was as if a weight had been lifted off her. Running back across the fields with Marnie, she felt as light as air. And even when Marnie had left her, and she was running home alone with the mushrooms, her face kept breaking into a smile for the pure joy of it.

On the corner she saw Sandra standing with two or three other children.

"Daft thing! Daft thing!" Sandra called when she saw Anna coming. "My mum says she's daft. Talks to herself, on the beach, she does. And frightened my little cousin ever so, when he wasn't doing nothing. Rushed up to him on the marsh, she did. My auntie said she looked fair daft, running like mad." She turned to a little boy in a blue plastic mackintosh who was standing beside her. "That's the girl, ain't it, Nigel?" He nodded his head solemnly. But Anna ran on, hardly noticing.

As she turned into the lane she could still hear Sandra calling after her, "Daft thing! Daft thing!" but she did not mind enough even to feel angry.

Chapter Seventeen

THE LUCKIEST GIRL IN THE WORLD

ANNA AND MARNIE met nearly every day now. They met on the beach, in the sandhills, and once they went mushrooming again in the early morning – but not in the same place. Marnie said no, she wasn't going so near that dreary old windmill, and when Anna asked her why, she pretended not to hear and raced on ahead.

As they crawled through the sandhills, searching for rabbits, or ran along the hard sand at low tide, they learned a lot about each other. Anna told Marnie all about home – she still found she could never tell her about the Peggs; when she was with her she always forgot all about them – and Marnie told Anna about her parents; her father, who was in the navy and often away, and her mother – the lady in the blue dress – who was more often in London than in Little Overton. Anna learned that for most of the time Marnie was alone at The Marsh House with her nurse and the two maids, Lily and Ettie.

"So you see, as long as they're happy gossiping in the kitchen or telling fortunes, I'm lucky because they don't even miss me and I can get out," Marnie told her, skipping about on the sand in an exaggerated way as if to show how happy and free she was. Anna could not help laughing. "And it's so lovely when the others come back! Mother's so beautiful – everyone tells her so – and I feel so proud. And Father's so handsome, and so kind. You've no idea how kind my parents are! Sometimes I think I'm the luckiest girl in the world."

"I think you are, too," said Anna.

"But now I've got you I'm even luckier!" Marnie flung her arms round Anna's waist. "You don't know how much I wanted someone like you to play with! Will you be my friend for ever and ever?" And she would not be satisfied until they had drawn a circle round them in the sand, and holding hands, vowed eternal friendship. Anna had never been so happy in her life.

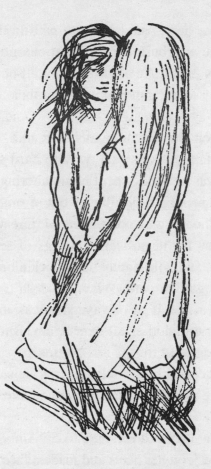

"It's funny," Marnie said one day, "but sometimes I feel as if I've been waiting for you to come here for years and years."

Anna looked up from the sand where, on hands and knees, she was diverting the course of a small stream. "I know," she said. "I feel as if I've been waiting to come here for years and years too. Which way shall I run this stream?"

"Bring it over here," said Marnie, patting the sides of a sandcastle she was building, "then it can go round our garden. This is going to be our house," she said, half laughing, half serious. "I'm making it for us to live in, just you and me."

They were on the far side of the marsh, where sea lavender and marsh weeds gave way to hard sand. Here, when the tide was out, they spent hours altering the course of streams, and making tiny villages out of mud and sand. Even before a house was completed Marnie would start making a garden for it, collecting sprigs of sea lavender to make bushes, and wild harebells to stick along the sides of each minute garden path. When, next day, they found the tide had washed it all away, she was undismayed and would start on another all over again. But Anna was always a little regretful for the lost houses.

"We'll live here all by ourselves," Marnie said, shaping the top to make a roof. "And we won't have any maids either."

"Tell me what Lily and Ettie are like," Anna said.

Marnie sat back on her heels and made a face. "All right, I suppose. Lily's quite nice. She makes chips and brings them to me in bed sometimes. But Ettie's not so nice. She's bad tempered, and she likes frightening people."

She made a chimney pot out of wet sand and balanced it on the roof. Then she said with a sigh, "They used to be quite fun, but not now. Ettie's got a friend in the army who used to write to her – she was quite jolly then – but I think he's stopped now. Secretly, I *believe* he writes to Lily instead, but I'm not sure. So now Ettie's terribly cross and ugly. She and Lily had a fight one day in the kitchen, and when Nan came down she found them crying and Lily said Ettie'd pulled her hair out, and Ettie said Lily'd stolen her boyfriend. It was quite frightful." She looked at Anna with wide eyes, then picked up her trowel again.

"Go on," said Anna. "What happened then?"

"Well, they were screeching at each other, and Nan said if they didn't shut up she'd see they got their notice – that meant she'd tell Mother when she came back and they'd have to go. But Nan doesn't want Ettie to go because she tells good fortunes in the tea leaves. And I don't want Lily to go because she tells me stories sometimes, when she brings me the chips in bed. So I said, 'Oh, no, don't make Lily go!' and that was silly, because Nan found out I was listening – I was hiding on the stairs, you see—" She broke off and shivered.

"So what?" said Anna.

"She was terribly angry." There was a pinched look on Marnie's face that Anna had not seen before. She was curious.

"Why, what did she do?"

"What she always does. You won't tell, will you? You mustn't." Anna shook her head. "She took hold of my arm, very tightly so it pinched and said I wasn't to dare tell when they came back, and she'd know if I did, and she made me promise. Then she took me upstairs and started brushing my hair. She always does that. She brushes terribly hard, and when she says, 'You're not to tell, do you understand?' she bangs the brush hard on my head so that it really hurts. Sometimes she winds my hair round and round on it, so it makes tangles – then she can go on brushing them out. She does that so no-one can say she's hurting me on purpose, you see? But I know. Sometimes it makes me cry like anything, it hurts so."

Anna was horrified. "But surely she wasn't doing that when I saw you?"

"Oh, no, there wasn't any reason then. It's only when she's cross, or to make sure I don't tell about anything."

"And do you ever tell?"

Marnie shook her head. "Not now. I used to when I was little, by mistake, and then I wouldn't remember what it was I was being punished for!" She laughed. "Come on, let's get on."

She jumped up and began planning the garden, talking all the while, but Anna was not attending. Marnie shook her by the shoulders. "Anna! Please, let's make our garden. You can make the paths with these shells, and we'll have a lawn and flower beds at the back instead of that dreary old sea—"

"What!" Anna was surprised. "Don't you like the sea? I've always thought you were so lucky having it come right up to the house like that."

"I'd rather have a garden," said Marnie. "There's one at the front, of course, but that's different. It's the drive, and Pluto's there. I'd like a proper garden with grass and flowers."

"The front?" Anna was puzzled. "Isn't that the front that looks out on to the staithe?"

Marnie stopped drawing flower beds in the sand and looked round at her in surprise. "The front? How could it be, you goose? How do you suppose people could come when the tide's up? Did you imagine everyone came like you did, in my little boat?"

She laughed, and Anna who had imagined just that, felt foolish. She realised now that of course it could not be so. She was surprised she had not thought of it before.

"They've changed my room to the back so I shan't be disturbed," Marnie went on. "At first it felt as if I was being shut away, but now I like it. After all, if I'd looked out on the front I'd never have seen you. Imagine it!"

"But tell me—" Anna was trying to work it out, "where does the front come out?"

"Along the main road, goosey. Beyond Pritchetts." Pritchetts was the old village shop, now derelict and deserted.

Anna thought hard, trying to visualise that part of the road, then remembered the high brick wall that ran along one side, with the tall iron gates halfway along. She had looked through them one day and seen a dark drive, bordered with yew trees, curving away to the left.

"It looks so different," she said slowly, "I never thought…"

But Marnie was not listening. "Just think if I'd gone on looking out at that dreary drive, and never known you were down on the staithe!" She spoke almost as if she were a prisoner.

"But you'd have come out," said Anna.

"Perhaps." Marnie sighed. "But I wouldn't have watched out for you, the way I do now, because I wouldn't have known you were there. I have to be up in my room a lot. I've lessons to do, for one thing." She shook her shoulders impatiently and picked out some bright green seaweed from the pile they had collected. "Don't let's talk about such things! Look, this shall be for the grass. Come on, why are you so dull?"

Anna was turning over in her mind all she had heard. "What did you mean about not being disturbed?" she asked.

"Just that," said Marnie. "They've put me away at the back of the house so I shan't be disturbed. So I can sleep quietly."

"Couldn't you before?"

Marnie shook her head. "I used to wake up in the middle of the night, when they'd had a party and were all going home. And I used to hear Pluto barking. I told you about that, didn't I?" She lowered her voice. "Sometimes he barks in the night, and I used to hear him and wake up frightened. I know it's all right really. He's got a chain on, so he can't get loose, but…"

She threw some more shells over to Anna, as if she wanted to change the subject. "Here, you make a path with those, then I'll plant the fruit trees, shall I? Come on, dreamy!"

They worked at the little house until the sun was quite low in the sky and there was an orange light reflected in the pools on the marsh. Anna was quiet on the way home. When Marnie asked her why, she said, "I've been thinking – you're supposed to be lucky – I mean you *look* lucky, and you have everything anyone could want – but you're not really, are you?"

"But of course I am!" Marnie was amazed. "I'm terribly lucky. What ever are you talking about?"

They had rounded the bend and come in sight of The Marsh House. "Oh, look! The lights are on. That means they've come!" Marnie pointed eagerly and Anna saw that the windows were all lit up.

"That's only the reflection of the sunset," she said.

"No, they've come! And Edward will be there." Marnie broke into a run, leaping over the streams and running so lightly over the boggy patches that Anna was soon several yards behind.

"Who's Edward?" she panted, struggling to keep up.

Marnie called back over her shoulder. "You know, the boy you saw – at the party. He's sort of a cousin of mine, and he's coming to stay."

Anna dropped behind. It was no use trying to keep up and there seemed no point now. But at the next stream Marnie had stopped after all and was waiting for her.

"I forgot to tell you he was coming," she said. "I'd even forgotten myself." She leaned forward a little, as if she were talking to a much smaller child, and her voice became coaxing. "Darling Anna, you know I'd *much* rather be with you. But Edward *is* my cousin, and he's quite nice. I must run now." She put her cheek against Anna's for a second, then ran on.

Anna had to be satisfied with that. Marnie loved her best, and would rather be with her. That was all she had wanted to hear. She paddled across the creek and saw that the windows of the house were in darkness after all. But that did not mean they had gone away; only that they were round the other side.

She thought of the dark drive and the forbidding front entrance on the main road. Edward, and all the other guests, were welcome to that, she thought happily. She and Marnie shared the side of the house that she liked best; the quiet, secret side that had seemed to recognise her when she first stood dreaming by the water, the side that looked as if it had been there for ever...

Chapter Eighteen

AFTER EDWARD CAME

EDWARD'S COMING MADE very little difference. Marnie did seem to like being with Anna best. Only, sometimes, when they had been on the beach as usual, she would jump up and say, "I must go. Edward will be wondering where I am." Then Anna would find it was time to go, too, and they would both turn back in the direction of the staithe.

Once Anna saw them walking together in the far distance along the beach, and for a moment she felt hurt. But a minute later Marnie came running up into the sandhills, alone; so pleased to see her that they might have been the only two people in the world.

"How quickly you can run!" said Anna. "You were miles away on the beach just now."

Marnie laughed. "That was *ages* ago, goosey. What a dreamy old thing you are! You must have been asleep."

That was quite probable. The weather had turned hot and Anna often dozed off when she was alone these days. Only when she was with Marnie did she feel really wide awake.

"This strong air really do seem to have gone to your head!" Mrs Pegg said, when Anna came home one evening with her eyelids drooping, heavy with sleep and sunshine.

Anna yawned, too tired even to reply. She had been out all day. She had wandered along the beach, waited in the sandhills, and dawdled home across the marsh at sunset. But she had not once seen Marnie. And yet she had thought they were to meet in the same place as yesterday.

Next day she went back to the same place and Marnie was there.

"Where have you *been*?" Marnie said. "I've been waiting ages for you."

"*I* waited ages for you yesterday," Anna said.

"Don't be silly, you couldn't have." Marnie pointed at the sand where some wild flowers lay scattered about. "Don't you remember? We left those here yesterday."

"That was the day before," Anna said. "Or was it the day before that?" She was not sure herself now. But the flowers still seemed quite fresh. Perhaps Marnie was right.

"Does it matter what day it was?" said Marnie. "Yesterday's gone, so has the day before. Don't let's waste today arguing about it."

But it happened again. It was exasperating to wait for hours in the chosen place, only to have Marnie pop up on the way home. Surely she used not to do this? Anna could not remember, but it began to feel as if Marnie was playing hide and seek with her.

"You promised to make a house today," Anna said once.

"I didn't promise. Why are you so cross?"

"I'm not cross, but you said you would. I've been waiting all day."

"Oh, poor you! But I can't be everywhere all the time. And I'm here now. Come on, let's be friends."

But Anna did not feel like being coaxed. "It isn't fair," she said. "I need you more than you need me."

"Nonsense. I need you, too, but you don't understand – I'm not free like you are. Don't let's quarrel, darling Anna!" Then Anna's resentment melted away, and they were happy again.

One day, wandering in the sand dunes, Anna came across a little shelter made of driftwood and marram grasses. It was big enough to crawl inside, and she crept in, thinking how pleased Marnie would be when she showed it to her.

But when she told her about it, Marnie said, "I know. Edward and I made it yesterday." Anna could not say anything at all then, she was so hurt and angry. For the first time since they had met, she put on her 'ordinary' face. But Marnie knew at once what it meant.

"Anna – Anna, I *was* going to show it to you, truly. Please don't look like that. Please don't go away from me."

And again Anna was coaxed back into forgiving her.

But she began to realise that she must not rely on Marnie too much. That if she was over-sure of meeting her, that would be the time she would not come. That it was almost as if Marnie was determined Anna should never take her for granted.

And yet sometimes they were as happy together as they had ever been.

One day, when Anna was lying on the farther dyke, near where they had first gone mushrooming, Marnie did her old trick of suddenly appearing in the grass beside her. Anna sat up, surprised. She had only chosen that place because she was sure she would not be seeing Marnie until later in the day.

"I thought you were going out with Edward," she said.

"I was, but I changed my mind. He decided he wanted to go and have a look at the windmill." Marnie settled down beside her. "What are you reading?"

Anna had not been reading, though she had a comic with her – the one Mrs Preston sent regularly. She handed it over. "Do you have this one?"

Marnie shook her head. "I'm not allowed them. Sometimes the maids have them – more grown-up ones, but they're comics just the same – and sometimes they let me read them, when they don't want me to be a nuisance and want to keep me out of the way."

"You can have that one if you like, but don't read it now. Tell me what the maids' ones are like." Anna did not think she had ever seen a grown-up's comic.

Marnie stretched herself on the grass beside her. "They're terribly exciting," she said, and her eyes grew dark and secret looking, "they're full of eerie mysteries – that's what they call them – all about nuns shut up in towers, and stolen babies, and wicked men. That's where I got the idea from that I might be really adopted."

"You talk as if you'd like to be," Anna said. "I didn't understand you when you said that before."

"Didn't you?" Marnie looked at her thoughtfully. "It's difficult to explain. It's only – well, I mean it would just *show* how good my parents are, wouldn't it. I mean they've given me everything – *everything*, and they've never even *hinted* that I might be adopted. But secretly, very secretly, I feel as if I am. Promise you won't tell?"

"Of course I won't. Anyway, who is there to tell? Go on telling me about the comics."

"Well, they have love stories and things." Marnie hesitated. "But I think love stories are sloppy, don't you?" Anna agreed. "And yet—" Marnie looked at her hopefully – "I do want to fall in love and get married when I'm grown up, don't you?"

Anna was not sure. "I don't know. I might fall in love with someone who didn't love me. I should think I would. I might keep dogs instead – have kennels."

"Oh, no, I should never do that!" Marnie turned the pages of the comic. "This is nicer than the grown-up kind. I'll keep it." She folded it and laid it aside. "I'll tell you another secret," she said seriously. "I don't want to grow up. Not ever. I shouldn't know how to be a proper grown-up, like Mother and her friends. I want to go on being like I am for ever and ever."

"But Marnie—" Anna was startled – "how can you say that? I should have thought—" she broke off, thinking of what Marnie had told her about her nurse bullying her.

"Yes, I know what you're thinking. But I'm used to that. And I know what to run away from if I'm frightened." She glanced quickly over her shoulder in the direction of the mill. "That horrible place, for one thing. But I don't know anything about being grown up, and no-one tells me."

"Why are you frightened of the mill?" asked Anna. "I wish you'd tell me."

Marnie looked away. "I don't know. I've always been scared of it. That's why I wouldn't go with Edward."

"Did you tell him you were frightened?"

Marnie shrugged, pretending to be indifferent. "I tried to, but he didn't understand. First he teased me, then he said if I was really frightened I ought to face up to it – that I couldn't go through life running away from things."

"It's easy to be brave for someone else," Anna said.

Marnie turned to her quickly. "Yes, isn't it? Edward's terribly serious sometimes." She smiled. "That's what I love about you, darling Anna. You don't keep telling me what I ought to do. I suppose I ought to go to the mill now, just to prove I can, but I've always been scared of it – ever since…"

"Since what?"

"Oh, it started ages ago. Ettie used to say, when I'd been naughty, 'They'll take you away and shut you up in the windmill with only the wind 'owling and then you'll be sorry.'" She was smiling but her face had the same pinched look as Anna had seen before. "I was only little then, but she made it sound terrible. Ettie's like that. She likes frightening people." She sighed, and shrugged her shoulders again.

"And once, when Father was going away, he asked me what I wanted and I said a red balloon, so he asked Nan to buy me one when she went into Barnham. But when she came back she'd got me a paper windmill instead – the kind that goes round and round in the wind. She said it would last longer. I was terribly disappointed, and I cried and cried, so then Nan got into a temper and she said, 'All right, my girl. If you don't like the windmill *I've* got you, we'll ask Ettie to take you to a better one.' And she told Ettie to take me for a walk, because she was tired after going into Barnham.

"I don't know if she really meant her to take me to the mill; perhaps she just meant to frighten me. But Ettie did. She dragged me all the way there, screaming, and I really thought she was going to have me shut up."

She smiled again, a tight, thin little smile. "It sounds silly now, I know, but I was terrified. Then, just when we got there, the sky went quite dark and there was a terrible thunderstorm. Ettie was frightened too, then, and I don't know whether that was better or worse!" She laughed, trying to shake off the ugly memory. "Ugh! Let's talk about something else."

But Anna was furious. "I never heard such a thing!" she said, outraged. "I *hate* Ettie. I wish she'd been struck dead."

Marnie looked startled. "What a funny girl you are. Why do you always look so shocked when I tell you things like that? Didn't anyone ever try to frighten you?"

"Not *grown-ups* – on *purpose*. Of *course* not!" Anna was nearly shouting with rage.

Marnie murmured, so low that it might almost have been the wind blowing over the grasses, "You are lucky. I wish I was you."

Anna turned to her, suddenly quiet. "That's what I said to you – last time we were here."

"Did you?"

"Yes, don't you remember? Oh, poor Marnie! I do love you. I love you more than any girl I've ever known." She put out a hand to touch Marnie's hair, then stopped in mid-air. "And that's what you said to me," she said slowly, with a surprised look on her face. "How funny, it almost seems as if we're changing places."

Chapter Nineteen

THE WINDMILL

ANNA SLIPPED OUT of the cottage at dusk that evening. Ever since Marnie had left her on the dyke earlier in the day, she had been thinking about the windmill. Now she turned along in that direction. She had never been there herself. Sam had kept saying at intervals that perhaps he would take her there but it had never happened. Now she had an idea.

She would go there by herself. She had never actually promised she would not. Then she would be able to find out whether there was really anything for Marnie to be so frightened about. She was fairly sure there was not, but she had to be sure. If she could say, next time she met her, there's nothing in it, I went there myself, then Marnie would believe her. Edward might have told her so, but Edward was different and he had called her a coward.

For once Anna would have something to give Marnie that Edward could not: the proof that her fears were groundless. She felt quietly excited with her idea.

It had grown dusk earlier than usual. The sky was overcast and a gusty wind blew about. "It looks as if weather's broken at last," Sam had remarked at tea-time. The water in the creek had been churned up into little choppy, grey-green waves, and Anna realised that even if the tide were right, Marnie would not have been able to take the boat out that night.

Now the seagulls were flying around inland, screaming angrily. They swooped over her head as she walked, and in the distance she could see them circling round the windmill, their wings white against the darkening purple sky. She began to wish she had thought of coming earlier in the day, but there was no turning back now. That would be really cowardly.

If she could go to the mill alone, now when it was nearly dark and she was half frightened herself, then tomorrow perhaps she would be able to persuade Marnie to let her take her there, by daylight, and show her round. It was probably the only place in Little Overton that Marnie did not already know. And this time Anna would have been there first!

The sky grew darker and something wet splashed on to her hand. She broke into a run and reached the mill as a few large drops of rain spattered down on to the dusty road.

She looked up and saw the mill towering above her. It was dark and enormous, and for a moment she had a terrible fear that it was leaning over towards her, and about to fall. Then dizzily, she searched for the door and pushed it open. It creaked horribly.

Inside it was quite dark. She stood, panting, waiting for her eyes to get used to the blackness. And at that moment, above the sound of her own heavy breathing, she heard another sound. It came from directly overhead. A gasp, followed by a sort of strangled choke. Someone was up there.

Anna stood dead still, too frightened to move. She remembered all Marnie's own panic, and the stories of ghosts, and people shut up in towers in the maids' comics, and suddenly she felt as if she had stopped breathing. She drew in her breath again, and it came in one long wheeze that seemed to go on and on.

There was a second's silence, then a panic-stricken whisper came from just over her head. "Who is it? Oh, *who* is it?"

Anna went hot with relief, though her legs still felt as if they were made of paper. "*Marnie*!" she said. "What ever are you doing up there? Goodness, you did frighten me!"

She could see more clearly now. A ladder went up from the floor, through a trapdoor to the floor above. She climbed up shakily. At the top Marnie was crouching on all fours. She clutched at her wildly and Anna scrambled up and over, on to the floor beside her.

"Marnie! What's the matter? What are you doing up here?"

Marnie's teeth were chattering so that she could hardly speak. "Oh, Anna, I'm so frightened! I heard someone tramping about outside and I thought I'd die of fright – then you came—" she began sobbing helplessly.

"But why are you here? Why did you come?"

Marnie gave a shuddering little sigh. "I hardly know now – I think I thought I'd be brave – Edward kept telling me I ought to be. Oh, Anna—!"

"Well, come on, let's get down and go home." Anna spoke briskly because she, too, was frightened. It was eerie up there and there was a horrible roaring noise. But Marnie made no attempt to move. "Do come!" Anna said again, urgently. "Oh, what is it – that terrible roaring noise?"

"It's the wind, 'owling. Isn't it ghastly!" Marnie said it perfectly seriously. Neither of them could possibly have felt like laughing.

Anna said, pulling at her, "Well, come on, let's get down. I think you were jolly brave to come. But let's get down now."

Marnie whimpered. "I can't, that's the thing—"

"Why not?"

Marnie pointed to the hole in the floor. Anna peered down over the edge, and saw what she meant. The ladder, which had been so easy to climb up, seemed now too far away to reach. They would have to step down into that dark, gaping hole.

She stepped back, shaking. Marnie's fear had gripped her, too.

"I've been here *ages*," Marnie sobbed, "half an hour at least – I was just going to run up here quickly – so I could say I'd done it, and then run home again. But when I looked down, I couldn't – I couldn't!"

"Don't *look* down, then," Anna said sharply. She got up and walked a few steps over to the wall, following it round with her hand, deliberately not looking down, or behind her. She needed the time to get over her own panic. Marnie followed her, shuffling across the floor on hands and knees. "What are we going to do?" she whimpered.

Anna ignored her, trying to recover her nerve. Then she turned round, and on hands and knees, groped her way back. Keeping her head up and her eyes turned away, she felt for the edge of the square opening and ran her hand along it. Then, still trying not to look down, she leaned forward and put her hand over the edge, feeling for the ladder. Twice she ran her hand along the full length of the side. Then she sat back on her heels, trembling.

"What is it?" asked Marnie. "What's the matter?"

"I can't find the ladder. It's gone."

"Oh, *no*!"

"It has. I've felt all along and it's not there. It must have slipped or something." Anna's voice was shaking.

"What are we to *do*?" Marnie sobbed, clinging to her. "Tell me what we're to do!"

"I don't know. Wait a minute and let me think." Anna shook her off. She had her own fear to deal with. But Marnie clawed at her, terrified. "Don't keep grabbing at me like that," Anna said gruffly, trying to keep her voice from trembling. "It makes it worse. I think we ought to try and be brave."

"I like that! You said yourself it's easy to be brave for other people. Now you're doing it."

"It isn't, and I'm not," Anna said. "I'm frightened, too. I'm only trying to think how not to be, so we can get down."

If only there was something to hold on to, she thought, to hold fast – and the words *Hold fast that which is Good* came into her mind, like the words of a nursery rhyme learned long ago. Then she remembered – it was the sampler on her bedroom wall. But that had an anchor on it. An anchor would be no good here. The only thing that would be good to hold on to here would be the ladder itself. But the ladder had gone. And Marnie was holding on to her!

She saw suddenly that she was all wrong. Of course the ladder was there – over on the other side. In her fear and confusion, she had moved round too far. She showed Marnie. There was nothing to be frightened of at all. They had only to hold on to the ladder and come down carefully, one at a time.

"Look, it's quite safe," she said. "You just hold fast on to the ladder and go down backwards. Shall I go first?"

"Oh, no! Don't leave me!" Marnie gasped.

"All right. You go first, then."

"But I can't – I *can't*! I told you."

Anna tried to persuade her, but it was useless. Marnie was now in such a state of terror that she was beyond reason. And every minute it was growing darker.

"I'm so cold – so very cold," Marnie kept saying, and her voice ended each time on a shuddering, shivering wail.

Anna tried everything. "Just leave go of me for a minute and *try*, Marnie. It's the ladder you want, not me. I can't do it for you. Please, please try. Or *shall* I go first?" But Marie would not hear of this.

It seemed hours later that Marnie gave a long drawn-out, shuddering sigh, and fell limply backwards. She had fallen asleep from sheer exhaustion. Anna gathered some loose straw from the floor and put it under her head.

Then she moved carefully over to the wall and sat with her back against it, watching her in case she should wake. Her head sank lower and lower, and in a moment she, too, was asleep.

Chapter Twenty

FRIENDS NO MORE

THE ROARING NOISE in Anna's ears grew louder and louder, and she woke with a start.

There were movements, voices, and the sound of heavy footsteps. She heard Marnie's voice whimpering faintly, "I thought you'd never come! Oh, Edward, I've been so frightened!" and opened her eyes. Then she remembered where she was.

She sat up, dazed and stiff with cold, and stared into the darkness. There was no-one there. The voices had receded, and she could hear only the noise of the wind and the scream of a seagull flying past overhead.

Marnie had gone, and she was alone in the mill!

Marnie had left her. She could think of nothing else but this one stark fact. She climbed stiffly down the ladder and ran out of that gloomy windmill, out into the wet, windy darkness, with this one thought hammering in her brain; that Marnie had left her. She had gone without her, and left her there alone. It was cruel, unforgivable.

She was too angry even to cry. She ran, gasping, along the road and through the fields, hardly noticing where she was going, the long wet grass whipping at her bare legs. Then she tripped, tried to save herself, and fell headlong into a ditch.

She pulled herself out again on hands and knees and lay sobbing weakly in the grass. Her foot was hurting. Each time she tried to move it, a hot stabbing pain ran across it. She lay still, thinking she would rest for a moment before trying to get up again. And knew no more.

Hours later Anna awoke. She was in her own bed. She turned her head and saw that a tray had been put down on the chair beside her. It held a boiled egg, a small brown teapot, and two slices of bread and butter. Mrs Pegg was pulling back the curtains. She turned and saw that Anna's eyes were open, and came over to the bed.

"There now, that's better. You had a nice sleep, didn't you? Now you sit up and eat your breakfast in bed like a

good maid. And don't you worry your head about nothing
– not till you've eaten that nice brown egg."

Anna moved, then winced with pain. She was stiff all
over. Mrs Pegg clicked her tongue. "There now, you've
caught a cold I shouldn't wonder. *And* hurt your ankle by
the looks of it. It looked all red and swollen to me when
they brought you in. That's what comes of staying out so
late and lying in the wet grass, you silly child," – but her
voice was gentle. "Don't you remember what happened?"

Anna did remember. Gradually it was coming back
to her. The windmill – Marnie in the windmill – and that
terrible roaring, moaning wind, going on and on. She
looked up at Mrs Pegg uncertainly. "You tell me," she
said. "I'm not sure."

"Well, you was in the fields, wasn't you? And you
must've got tired and laid down and gone clean off. We
was that worried Sam and me, not knowing where you
was, and it were blowing up real nasty. Then along come
Mr Pearce knocking on the door, saying he'd been going
by in his car and just happened to see you in the headlights
as he turned the corner. So he brought you right back to the
door." Anna had a faint memory of someone lifting her up
and carrying her, and the hum of a car engine, but nothing
more.

Mrs Pegg stood looking down at her thoughtfully. "That
were a silly thing to do, my duck. I can't think what come
over you. But there – what's done's done." She poured out

a cup of tea and pushed the tray a little nearer to the bed. "Now you eat your breakfast and just lay quiet, while I go and get dinner on. I thought we'd have a nice brown stew, seeing it's like it is." She glanced out of the window as a gust of wind tore round the house, rattling the frames. "One thing, you ain't missing nothing today. Sam's right, weather's broke and no mistake."

When Mrs Pegg had gone Anna allowed all the details of the night before to come flooding into her mind. Like a heavy weight, the memory of what Marnie had done descended on her. She felt sick at heart. Marnie had left her alone in the mill. Alone and frightened, in the dark. And Anna had thought she was her best friend!

At first it seemed as though Edward – or whoever it was had rescued Marnie – had left her behind on purpose. But then she remembered how she had been sitting, with her back against the wall, and realised he had probably never seen her. No-one would have expected her to be there. But how could Marnie have gone without even a word? Anna could never forgive her for that. And she would never trust anyone again.

The hurt inside her hardened. She pushed away the tray and lay down again. Then, turning her face to the wall, she closed her mind to everything.

Down in the scullery Mrs Pegg put on the onions to fry for the "nice brown stew" and turned them, sizzling, in the pan. Like Mrs Preston, she believed there was no hurt in the world that could not be cured by a good square meal. Soon the cottage was filled with the familiar, homely smell of frying onions. It escaped from the scullery, crept through the kitchen, sniffed along the bottom of the closed front-room door and wound its way stealthily up the crooked staircase, even under the door into Anna's bedroom. But even this – the most delicious, hungry-making smell in the world – was unable to rouse her. Anna slept on.

For two long days the wind roared round the house, and Anna stayed in bed. Her foot was not broken and, though still bruised and swollen, was getting better, but she had a heavy cold. She was better off where she was, Mrs Pegg said.

Anna could not have cared where she was. Nothing seemed to matter any more. Marnie, her only friend, was her friend no more.

On the third day she got up, pale and solemn, and Mrs Pegg, having settled her comfortably in an easy chair in the kitchen, left her to go shopping. Sam was asleep in his big armchair in the corner.

Anna looked out of the window with dull, heavy eyes. For the moment the wind had eased. It was raining still, but the sky looked brighter, and she could hear the gulls crying down by the creek. It seemed ages since she had been down there. Ages since Marnie had left her in the mill. Those two days in bed had seemed more like a hundred years, she thought bleakly.

Not that she wanted to see Marnie. There was no question of that. She had decided while she was in bed that she would never speak to her again. But she wanted Marnie to see her. She wanted her to look out of her window and see her down there on the staithe, and remember the mean, cruel thing she had done. If they met, Anna would not even look at her. But Marnie should not be allowed to forget her. You could not do things like that to people and then forget all about them, she told herself.

She would go down there now. She had been thinking about it long enough. She got up quietly, throwing aside the woollen shawl Mrs Pegg had laid over her legs, and crept out past Sam into the scullery, and out of the back door.

Outside the light seemed unusually bright, and the sudden freshness of the air almost took her breath away. She clung on to the railing for a moment. Then, feeling oddly shaky and unreal, she limped down the lane and turned towards the creek.

Chapter Twenty-One

MARNIE IN THE WINDOW

THE WATER LOOKED leaden. The tide was more than halfway in, and the staithe was deserted. Beyond the marsh a great dark purple cloud was coming in from the sea. Anna shivered and wished she had put on something warmer.

She went down to the water's edge. If Marnie were looking out of her window she could not fail to see her, she thought, walking slowly along, kicking at pebbles and stooping every now and then to pick up a stone, a feather – it did not matter what. She examined each closely, seeing

161

nothing, concerned only with being seen herself, and moved slowly along the shore.

It began to rain harder. The cloud had moved overhead, and she could hear the heavy raindrops spitting into the creek. She straightened her back, saw that she was now opposite The Marsh House, and involuntarily, before she had time to stop herself, glanced up at Marnie's window. Yes, she was there. Or was she? She looked back again quickly to make sure. And remained looking.

Marnie was in the window, staring out with an oddly twisted face – or was it the rain running down the glass that distorted it? Anna moved up the staithe, still staring, forgetting all her previous resolutions, and saw that Marnie was waving to her, calling out to her to come nearer. She was trying to tell her something.

She moved closer to the bank and stood looking up, not even noticing the rain which was now pouring down, or the wind which was whipping up the water into angry little waves; seeing only Marnie in her blue smock, pressed up against the glass. She was beating her hands on the window, and crying out in her old, loving, extravagant way, "Anna! Darling Anna!"

"What?" she shouted back.

"Anna! Oh, how I wish I could get to you! But I can't. They've locked me in. And they're sending me away tomorrow. I wanted to tell you – to say goodbye – but they wouldn't let me out.

"Anna—" she wrung her hands despairingly behind the glass – "please forgive me! I didn't mean to leave you all alone like that. And I've been sitting up here crying about it ever since. Say you forgive me!"

The words were almost carried away on the wind, and Marnie's face was nearly obscured by the rain that streamed in rivers down the outside of the window. But Anna heard and understood. It was almost as if the words were coming from inside herself, so clear they were in spite of the wind and the rain.

And suddenly all the bitter grudge she had been feeling against Marnie melted away. Marnie was her friend, and she loved her. Joyfully she shouted back, "Yes! Oh, yes! Of course I forgive you! And I love you, Marnie. I shall never forget you, ever!"

There was so much more she wanted to ask her; whether it was really true she was going away, and where? And would she be coming back? But the rain was falling now in blinding streaks, slantwise, whipping her hair across her wet cheeks and stinging her legs; and Marnie's face had become barely more than a pale smudge in the dark window.

Then, suddenly, as she stood there straining her eyes up to the house, she felt the shock of cold water swirling over her feet. She turned quickly and saw that the tide had come in behind her – a great mass of choppy, grey water, spreading wider and wider. Already the marsh was nearly covered.

She turned again to the window. Marnie's face had disappeared completely, blotted out by the blinding rain. But she waved wildly, trying to smile a goodbye, and pointing along the narrow strip of shore, which would soon be covered. And suddenly, as she looked, it seemed to her that the house was empty after all. That there was no-one behind any of those blank, staring windows. It looked like a house that had been empty a long time…

Sobbing, she turned away and plunged along towards the end of the bank where the road began. Already the strip of shore had disappeared and the water was pulling at her legs. The tide must have come in extraordinarily quickly, and it was still rising. She could feel the stones and sharp pebbles, and bits of sea wrack that lined the edge of the staithe, cutting into the soles of her feet. She tried to grasp the long grass on the bank, hoping to scramble up but it was too slippery to hold and she fell back again.

Gasping and sobbing, she plunged on, her legs heavy as lead as they pushed their way through the weight of the water. Already it was over her knees. Rain and tears poured down her cheeks, her clothes clung to her, limp and sodden, and her hair slapped across her face like bands of seaweed. She was icy cold and soaked through. Only her throat was parched and burning.

It came to her that she might be drowned if she could not reach the bank in time. The water was now rising up her thighs, and she was only halfway there. But *she would not be drowned.* People could do what they liked to her, but nobody could make her be drowned if she didn't want to be. She *must* reach the corner.

Her mind leapt ahead. In her imagination she saw herself hobbling home dripping, and creeping upstairs to her own room. She had been nearly drowned, but nobody should know. Nobody had ever known anything that was important to her. Not how she had felt about being paid for, about being treated as if she was different, about people not knowing what they were going to do with her. Not even about Marnie, her first, very own best friend. And now she had gone! She sobbed at the thought, stumbled, and fell, choking, into the grey swirling water.

Chapter Twenty-Two

THE OTHER SIDE
OF THE HOUSE

ANNA *HAD* NEARLY been drowned, and somebody did know about it. Wuntermenny coming up the creek in his boat, saw her fall just as he rounded the bend, and, thinking more quickly than he had ever thought in his life before, he steered straight towards her. In a moment he was up to his waist in water, had caught her up in his arms, and was wading towards the shore.

Mrs Pegg said afterwards that never would she forget

the shock of it, when Wuntermenny came tramping through the scullery just as she was unloading her shopping bag. She'd turned round and there they both were, pouring half the creek over her clean kitchen floor without so much as a by-your-leave.

More than that – Wuntermenny had then made the longest speech anyone had ever heard come out of his mouth. "Little lass were near drownded," he had said. "Lucky that were blowing up nasty, so I come back and see'd her blundering about in water. Tide's flooding uncommon fast." Then he had laid her down on the sofa and said, "Heaviest catch I ever made, I reckon," just as if the poor little lass were a cod fish, and stumped out again before ever Mrs Pegg could draw breath.

But that was later. For many days Mrs Pegg had neither time nor inclination to talk about it at all. And it was not until long after that she took to telling the tale as if it had been wonderfully exciting, almost funny, instead of quite terrible.

Anna was ill for a long time. She had feverish nightmares and woke screaming, and every bone in her body ached. But always there was someone there to break the terrible dream, and soothe her, or give her a drink. Once, to her surprise, it was Mrs Preston who was bending over her in a dressing-gown, holding a glass of water to her cracked dry lips.

"Auntie," she croaked, and tried to smile.

Mrs Preston patted her hand and laid her gently back on the pillow. "Go to sleep, my pet," she murmured.

Even in her half-delirium Anna thought, can she mean me? How strange. She had never heard her use such a term of endearment before. Then she did as she was told and fell into a dreamless sleep.

Gradually she grew better and was able to get up a little. Mrs Preston, who had been staying at the cottage helping Mrs Pegg, began to talk of going home again. "Uncle" needed her, she said. But the doctor thought Anna should stay on if possible, as the air here was so good for her.

"I'm wondering how you feel about it, dear?" Mrs Preston, perched on the edge of Anna's bed, was casting anxious, sideways glances at her. "Would you *rather* come home with me?" Anna did not know what to say. "You have been happy here, haven't you?" Mrs Preston went on. "Mrs Pegg says you have, and she and Sam want you to stay on. But of course I should hate to leave you here if you weren't. What would you *like* to do?"

"Did Mrs Pegg say she wanted me to stay?" Anna asked incredulously.

"Yes, she did. She said they both liked having you about the place. But I wanted *you* to choose."

Anna sensed a certain anxiety in the way Mrs Preston waited for her answer. "I'll stay, then," she said.

Mrs Preston got up at once and said brightly, "That's settled then. I'll go and tell them."

Considering how relieved she must have been at her choosing to stay, Anna thought it odd that Mrs Preston looked so suddenly upset when they parted. Just for a moment she held her tightly in her arms and mumbled something that sounded almost like, "wish you were coming – never mind, perhaps some day we'll—" Then, without finishing the sentence, she let go and pretended to be buttoning up Anna's cardigan, which was buttoned already.

Anna had just time to give her a quick, unexpected hug before Sam shouted up the stairs that the station bus was coming round the corner. Then she was gone.

Before long Anna was out and about again, and life at the cottage had settled back into its old routine. But for Anna things were not the same.

Since her illness a shutter seemed to have come down between her and everything that had happened to her just before she was nearly drowned. It seemed now as if it had all happened a long time ago. Sometimes she almost felt as if she were seeing Little Overton for the first time. Then she would remember Marnie.

Marnie had gone. There was no doubt about it. As soon as she saw The Marsh House again, Anna knew for sure. She stood for a long while gazing at it, wondering what was different, and could find nothing specific. The house just looked empty. She was not surprised. She had known in her heart that she would never see Marnie again. But secretly she mourned for her.

Another thing that was different was that there were more people about. The first of the summer visitors were beginning to arrive; families with babies, and toddlers who splashed about almost naked in the shallow water on the sandy side of the creek. She helped two of them build a sandcastle one day, while their mother talked to a friend higher up the beach. She had never played with such little children before, and almost enjoyed it.

Coming across the marsh at low tide one afternoon, she found an old lady sitting on a camp stool, sketching. She stood behind her for a moment, quietly watching, and saw that she was painting the staithe and The Marsh House.

The lady turned and glanced up at her, and smiled. Instead of slinking away, as she would previously have done, Anna found herself smiling back. The lady was not so old after all – only about Mrs Pegg's age.

"Do you think it's like it?" she asked, pointing to the house in her picture.

Anna leaned forward, studying it carefully, and said yes, it was.

"I love that old house, don't you?" said the woman.

"Yes," Anna said.

The woman turned back to her painting. Anna waited, wondering if she would turn round again, but she didn't, so she crept quietly away. But she was pleased and felt as if she had made friends with someone just by not running away.

She went along the main road past Pritchett's one morning, and coming to the front entrance of The Marsh House was surprised to find the iron gates wide open. She went in a little way and heard a sound of hammering, then following the bend in the drive she came in full view of the house, and stopped and stared.

She had never imagined it would look like this. It was just as attractive as the old house by the water. For some reason she had always thought of the front as if it were some quite different place. Now, for the first time, she realised what she must always have known really; they were two sides of the same house. And this side was, if anything, even more attractive. It had a warm, welcoming look which she had never expected.

More surprising still – all the windows were open. The frames had been newly painted, and the sound of hammering was coming from one of the upper rooms.

Beside the front door, also half open, a crimson rose bush sprawled up the wall and hung in clusters over the porch.

As she stood there, staring, a workman came round the side of the house carrying a ladder over his shoulder. Before she had time to run, he had seen her and called out, "Who was you wanting to see? They ain't here yet."

Anna stood with her mouth open, unable to find an answer.

The man laid down the ladder and came nearer. "What is it, love?" he asked jokingly. "Ain't you ever see'd a man with a ladder before?" He jerked his head back towards the house. "Cleaning up the old place a bit, that's what we're doing. Did you wonder what all the banging was? That's the carpenter, that is, mending holes in the floorboards and suchlike."

He paused and looked at her more closely. "Why, ain't you the little-old-girl from up at Peggs'? My, but ain't you growed! You're twice the size you was when last I see'd you."

"Yes," said Anna. "I was in bed, and you always grow a lot then."

"Oh, ah! Of course." The man nodded his head slowly. "You was nearly drownded, wasn't you?" He clicked his tongue sympathetically. "I heared about that. Well, maybe things'll be a bit more lively for you soon, when the family comes down."

"What family?" Anna faltered.

"The family what's bought the old place. That's why we're doing it up. Nice people they are. A Mr Lindsay and his wife. They come down and looked at it Easter time. Said it was just the thing."

Anna said, in a small, uncertain voice, "What – do you know what happened to the other family?"

The man looked blank. "Which family was that?"

"The one that used to be here?" Her voice had grown even more uncertain.

The man shook his head. "There wasn't no other family that I ever heard of. Not since my time, any road. But I ain't been in Overton all that long."

"Oh. Thank you."

The man moved back towards the house, and Anna walked slowly away. At the bend in the drive she looked back.

Two sides of the same house... One facing out on to the main road, the other looking back over the water... And so strongly had she been attracted to the backward-looking side that she had even, for a while, mistaken it for the front. She wondered how she could have been so silly. But then, the gates had always been closed before, so how could she have known?

She heard the sudden sound of a car turning in at the entrance, and darted in among the dark yew trees. An old packing case lay there, rotting on the ground, and she ducked down behind it until the car had passed. She heard the car draw up to the front door and the engine stop, then she slipped round the back of the packing case and out on to the drive.

She gave a quick backward glance as she ran towards the gates, and saw that it was not a packing case after all. It was an ancient dog kennel lying rotting on its side.

Chapter *Twenty-Three*

THE CHASE

ANNA STOOD IN the sandhills and stared. In the distance, on the stretch of sand that led across to the marsh, she was sure she had just seen five small, dark figures. They were running, jumping, separating, then joining together again, and growing smaller every minute.

She stood staring until the sun in her eyes forced her to look away for a moment. When she looked back they were gone.

She turned away. For a moment she had been quite startled. Those five small figures reminded her of the imaginary family she had once thought lived in The Marsh House. But that had been before she met Marnie. Now she knew better.

She lay down on her back in a hollow, feeling suddenly lonely, and wept for Marnie. The sad, long-ago sound of the gulls crying in the distance brought real tears now, and they fell from the corners of her eyes, trickling down the sides of her neck and wetting her hair before they sank into the sand.

But even as she wept, a new and delicious sadness was creeping over her. The sadness one feels for something enjoyed and now over, rather than for something lost and never found again. A sandpiper flew overhead calling, "Pity me!" but its cry was now like a little lament for Marnie rather than an empty pity for herself.

Comforted by her own tears, she lay there until the sun had dried them, then she rolled over and ate a ginger biscuit that had fallen from her pocket into the sand. She ruffled the back of her hair and let the sun dry that too.

Soon she heard children's voices, and got up. Now, halfway through July, the beach was no longer her own. Small children came searching for crabs among the rocks, and scattered in the sandhills family parties sat picnicking, invisible until one stumbled upon them, but clearly audible when the wind was in the right direction. Lunch-time was over, soon more people would be coming down to the beach.

She climbed to the highest point of the dunes, and shading her eyes with her hand, looked again across the stretch of sand towards the marsh.

Yes, there they were again. It was quite extraordinary. Five small, dark figures – coming nearer this time – hopping, running, zig-zagging across the sands towards the sea. Five dark figures in navy blue jeans and jerseys. This was what she had been half expecting, half fearing to see.

They were not real. She knew that. No-one in the village had ever seen that imaginary family of hers. She had asked Mrs Pegg again, and Mrs Pegg had said no, even Miss Manders hadn't seen them – she'd asked her specially – and Miss Manders knew everybody.

Anna stood looking for one more minute, then moved down into another hollow, and put them out of her mind. She was not going to be trapped into believing they were real just because she kept thinking she saw them. But a few moments later, hearing voices again, she peeped over the tops of the grasses and saw that they were coming nearer. They were winding their way through the sandhills straight towards her.

She leapt up and ran full tilt down the slope into a smaller, deeper hollow, and waited. When she lifted her head and looked round again, there was no sign of them anywhere.

But going home in the late afternoon, she saw them again. She was walking back along the bed of the creek, paddling through the shallows as the tide was low, when, looking over towards the marsh, she saw the five small, dark figures silhouetted against the sky, walking in single file along a raised bank. She stood and stared. And at that moment, the one at the end, lagging a little behind the others, turned and looked straight towards her, then stopped dead.

Anna ran, but not before she had time to see the same small figure turn sideways and start plunging at a right angle across the marsh, down towards the place where, only a moment ago, she herself had been standing. She hid under the bank at the edge of the marsh and worked her way backwards in a crouching position. Then, having rounded the bend in the creek, she sat down under the bank for at least ten minutes.

When she crept cautiously out again there was no-one to be seen.

Next day the same thing happened again. She saw them, ran from them, then saw them again. It was the same the day after, and the day after that. It became like a game, seeing them without being seen, and gradually it developed into a chase.

They had seen her, she was sure. One in particular, a girl with long brown hair, neither the oldest nor the youngest, always seemed to catch sight of her even when the others did not. She would stop and look back, scanning the sandhills as if actually searching for her. And Anna, if she had grown bold too soon, would be caught out on hands and knees, looking over the top of her hollow, watching them go away. She always ducked down quickly, but she had an idea the brown-haired girl saw her every time.

The Chase

She grew to know them by sight. There was a big boy of about fourteen, probably the oldest, then a fair-haired girl with plaits, then the long brown-haired girl. She looked a little younger than Anna. Then there was another boy, perhaps seven or eight, and a little one, almost a baby.

The girl with the plaits was often with the youngest, holding his hand or carrying him through the shallows. Then the two boys would be together and the brown-haired girl would be on her own. Or sometimes the two oldest would pair off and the two younger ones be together. But whichever way it was, the brown-haired one would, more often than not, be separated a little from the others, either trailing behind or dancing along on her own.

She is the one I would like best, thought Anna, although she's younger than me. The older one looks too sensible and grown-up, though she's awfully kind to the baby. Then she would shake herself, realising she was thinking of them as real people. And they could not be real. She herself had imagined them in the beginning, before she had even met Marnie, and no-one else had ever seen them.

But real or not, they continued to be there and, in spite of herself, Anna found it exciting. She took to skirting the edge of the dunes rather than crossing an empty stretch of beach, feeling that if she went out in the open, five pairs of eyes might be watching her from the sandhills. She went down to the beach earlier in the mornings and watched from the topmost point of the sandhills so that she could see them crossing the marsh. One day, to her horror, she found they had come by boat when she was not looking, and before she knew it they were almost upon her, coming up from behind.

She ran, her heart thumping, and escaped them again. She had the advantage of them, knowing all the dips and hollows of the sandhills by heart, but that had been a near thing.

It was like being chased by your own imagination, she thought, as she lay panting in a hollow. But what of that? They were not bogeys. And yet she was half frightened of the chase. It was an exciting game, until she was in danger of being caught. Then she ran in panic as if she were a wild animal being hunted.

She peered through the marram grass and saw them moving away in the opposite direction. Immediately, instead of relief, she felt disappointment.

She came out and sat deliberately in the open, knowing that if they turned round they would see her at once. It was an exciting risk that she had to take even though her heart was in her mouth. Then the very thing she feared, and yet courted, happened. They did turn round. She heard one of them shout, "There she is!" and they began running towards her. But now she was unable to move! She felt as if she were rooted in the sand. And every second they were coming nearer! Then, when it was almost too late, she found her legs again. She sprang up and ran like the wind, away over the dunes until she had nearly reached the far end where the hillocks levelled out and became flat sand. She plunged headlong into the last remaining hollow and burrowed her way down into the fine, warm sand.

Her heart was thumping in her ears and she was trembling with excitement. Don't let them catch me! she kept saying, over and over in her head. Don't let them catch me! Still gasping for breath, she divided the grasses and peeped out. Everything was still. The sea showing between the grass stalks was a deep, deep blue. A drowsy peace had settled over everything.

Then the peace was shattered. There was a sudden scrambling noise, a shout of triumph, and five figures rose up out of the grasses all around her. She was surrounded!

"Got you!" one of them shouted, and her ankle was seized in a strong, warm hand.

Chapter Twenty-Four

CAUGHT!

"GOT YOU!" THE voice said again.

Anna struggled feebly then lay still. She wormed her way over on to her back, her ankle still firmly held, and stared up at the big boy bending over her, trying all the while to put on her ordinary face. But it would not work. The face looking down into hers was so merry, so absurd in its attempts to look ferocious, that she smiled in spite of herself.

"So you *are* real," she said, still half surprised.

The girl with the plaits came round and bent down to look at her. "That's funny, that's just what we said about you, that you weren't real! Let go of her, Andrew. We've got her now."

"Promise you won't run away?" he demanded.

Anna nodded. "Not yet, anyway."

Andrew let go and she sat up, rubbing her ankle. "I say, I'm sorry about that," he leaned forward to examine the red marks left by his fingers. "It doesn't hurt, does it?" Anna shook her head. "But you'd led us such a dance we couldn't have let you go, now could we?"

"Priscilla saw you first," said the girl with the plaits. "That's her." She pointed to the brown-haired girl who was looking on, silent and wide-eyed. "I'm Jane, and that's Matthew over there, and this is Roly-poly." She patted the toddler who was busily burying himself in sand.

"His real name's Roland," said Matthew, "but we call him Roly-poly for long."

"And that's Matthew's favourite joke," said Andrew.

"Scilla kept saying she saw you," said Jane with the plaits, "and we all thought she was imagining you until we saw you ourselves. I don't believe she thinks you're quite real even now!"

Andrew pinched Anna's calf. "But that's real enough. See, Scilla? – she's as real and solid as you are. Serves you right for making up stories about imaginary girls." He turned to Anna again. "By giminy, aren't you *brown*! Have you been down here long? What's your name?"

"Anna."

"Oh." He sounded almost disappointed, then laughed. "We've been making up the most glamorous names for you, Marguerite and Marlene and Madeleine—"

"And Melanie and Marianne and Marietta," put in Jane.

"And Mary Anne," said Matthew.

"Mary Anne's not glamorous," said Jane.

"But why all beginning with M?" Anna asked curiously.

"Scilla started it," Jane said. "She was sure it did."

The girl, Scilla, looked at her sideways, saying nothing.

"She's got a secret name for you, but she won't tell anyone what it is," said Andrew, laughing. Priscilla, who had still not said anything, turned away and began drawing zigzags absentmindedly in the sand with the tip of her big toe. "Will you tell Anna?" Andrew asked her, "now you've met her?"

Priscilla shook her hair over her face, not answering.

"Don't tease her," Jane said. But already Priscilla was moving away, down towards the beach.

They got up and wandered in the same direction, talking all the time. They told Anna they were lucky, having left school a week before the end of term so they could come down to the new house with their parents. The workmen were still in and their mother was busy all day, trying to get the place in order. That was why they had Roly-poly with them all the time, to keep him out of the way. Their father was coming down at the weekend. Wasn't Little Overton a super place? Their parents had come down at Easter and seen the new house, but the children had not seen it until half-term, after it had been bought. Then they had all come down for the day.

Anna knew that the new house they were talking about was The Marsh House. It seemed strange to hear it called "new". It seemed strange, too, to be walking out in the open again, unafraid of being seen! Now, feeling suddenly free, she ran down the sandy slope on to the wide stretch of beach and began turning cartwheels, one after the other.

The others immediately did the same. Even Roly-poly had a try, but he was too fat. They gave him a wheelbarrow race instead, but he sank in the middle and collapsed, squealing with delight. Jane persuaded him to turn head over heels by himself, and the others began walking on their hands and practising handstands. Only Priscilla stayed down by the water's edge, dancing along on her own.

Anna paused to watch her. She was dancing along with an odd sideways movement, twisting this way and that, one foot pointing in the sand. Anna moved nearer and saw that she was still drawing with the tip of her big toe, a long, zig-zagging line that stretched along the smooth, hard sand. She looked so intent and preoccupied that Anna was curious.

"What is she doing?" she asked Jane, who had come up beside her.

"Who, Scilla?" Jane glanced along the shore. "Oh, playing some secret game of her own, I expect. She's full of secrets lately – always inventing ridiculous things. That's why we thought she was imagining *you*!"

She ran to rescue Roly who was staggering down towards the sea. "Here, Roly-poly, time to go home, darling! Come and let's find Mummy."

It was time for them to go. They drifted back towards the sandhills to collect their belongings.

"Will you be down tomorrow?" Andrew asked, stowing their shoes and jerseys into a haversack. Anna said she would. "Mind you turn up, then! No skulking in the reeds like a cross-eyed nymph."

"How dare you? I'm not cross-eyed!" Never had Anna been so happy to be called names!

"No, perhaps not, but you ought to be, after squinting at us through the grass for so long! We began to think we were. First we'd see you in one direction, then we'd turn round and see you somewhere else. Scilla was convinced you were a— what did she call her, Jane?"

Matthew shouted, "A bantam!"

"That's it. – No, not a bantam, half-wit! – That's a hen. A phantom, that's what she called you. An eerie phantom! Goodness knows what she's been reading lately." He hoisted the haversack on to his shoulders. "Goodbye, then. See you tomorrow." He set off towards the marsh.

"See lou to-mollow," said Roly, staggering about under an enormous yawn. Jane bent down and picked him up.

"And the day after," said Matthew, grinning at Anna and helping to hoist Roly on to his sister's back.

"Andy after," said Roly, his eyelids drooping.

Jane looked round. "Where's Scilla? Is she still on the beach? Tell her we've gone on, will you Anna. Roly's so tired." Priscilla came running up at that minute. "Oh, there you are, do hurry!" said Jane. "The boys have gone on."

Anna helped Priscilla find her shoes, already half buried in the fine sand. "What were you doing down there?" she asked, still curious.

"Nothing special – just thinking," said Priscilla with a shy, secret smile. "You can go and see if you like."

She ran off after Jane, then turned and waved her hand and continued walking backwards, waving, until they were almost out of sight.

Anna heaved a deep, happy sigh, and looked around. The beach was suddenly quiet. Every one else had gone home, too. She went down to the water's edge again. But there was nothing to be seen. No pictures drawn in the sand, no writing, not even her own name. Nothing but the marks of Priscilla's bare feet and that long, broken, zigzagging line. She did not know what she had expected to see, but she was faintly disappointed.

The tide was beginning to come in. It was a soft, hazy evening, and she stood dreamily watching the little ripples running up the sand until they reached the edge of the zigzagging line. One of them ran right through it, breaking it up, so that when the water receded only the shape of one large M was left on the sand.

M for Marnie, she thought, staring at it. But of course

– they had all been Ms. The broken, zigzagging line had been a long row of capital M's stretching as far as Priscilla had gone. Why hadn't she seen it before? M for Madeleine, M for Marguerite, M for Melanie and the rest, she thought, smiling as she remembered the long string of glamorous names they had invented for her. No wonder plain "Anna" had seemed a little disappointing!

How strange it was, she thought, as she plodded home across the marsh, the way things changed without your even noticing it. Marnie had been real and they had not. Now they were real and Marnie was not. Or was it she who had changed?

Chapter Twenty-Five

THE LINDSAYS

ANNA COULD HARDLY remember Marnie now. Only sometimes at night, when the moon shone in at the low window of her room, and she was lying awake, she would remember her in flashes, like pictures – Marnie running in the sand dunes, Marnie in the boat at dusk, and Marnie crying and crying in the window on that last terrible morning. Then she would cry a little herself, and think, Oh, I'm so glad I forgave her! Even if she wasn't real, I'm so glad! And she would fall asleep comforted.

But during the day Marnie was no more than a ghost of a memory – and soon she ceased to be even that.

There was no doubt about the Lindsays being real. They were so lively, and there were so many of them. Priscilla was the one Anna found most difficult to get to know. She had a way of wandering off alone, even in the middle of a game, as if she had something important to think about. And yet, when she was with the others, she would sit gazing at Anna as if she would like nothing more than to be friends with her. It was almost as if she were waiting for something, some sign from Anna, before she could treat her in the same casual, friendly way as the others did.

One afternoon, a few days after she had first met them, Anna was helping Roly-poly sail his little boat in a shallow pool. They had been playing cricket on the beach. Now the game was over, and Andrew and Matthew had gone off shrimping. Priscilla had gone farther down the beach by herself, and now Anna saw that she was kneeling on the sand, apparently arranging something in front of her with great care.

Every now and again Anna saw her pick up something from beside her and add it to whatever lay in front of her, then she would sit back on her heels and look at it consideringly, with her head on one side. What could she be doing? Anna would have liked to wander down and find out, but she could not leave Roly alone. Jane was up in the sandhills, collecting their things together and Anna had promised to look after him until she came back. She stood up, wondering whether she could take him by surprise and pick him up and run with him, before he had time to protest. And at that minute Jane came running back.

"Thanks awfully for looking after him, Anna. You are a dear. I'd better take him home now." She glanced around the beach. "Where are they all?"

"The boys are shrimping down by the creek."

"Oh, then we'll give them a shout as we go by."

"Shall I go and tell Scilla?"

"No, no need. I'll leave a note with our things. I say, do come back with us! Come and have tea. Mummy won't mind. She likes us to bring people."

Anna hesitated, but Jane said, "Oh, no, it won't be a polite tea – just buns and things. Do come!"

"I think I'd like to—" Anna lingered a moment, glancing towards Priscilla.

"Oh, don't mind her," said Jane, "she hates being interrupted. She'll come when she's ready. We'll leave a note." She glanced at Anna quickly. "She isn't unfriendly or anything. Don't think that. It's just that she likes mooning about by herself."

"Oh, no, I didn't think she was."

They went up to the sandhills, left the note, and walked back together with Roly-poly between them, shouting to the boys as they passed them in the distance.

It seemed strange to Anna to be going along the footpath at the top of the bank, and in at the side door of the old house. But once she was inside it seemed like a new house altogether. The passage was filled with Roly's pushchair and tricycle, and there were bicycles leaning up against the wall. In the hall there were crates of books, half unpacked, and various pieces of furniture piled up, one on top of the other.

"You see, we're still not properly unpacked," said Jane. She ran to find her mother.

Mrs Lindsay was like Jane, only plumper, and she had Andrew's humorous grey eyes. She said hello to Anna as if she knew her already and was glad to see her. Yes, of course Anna could stay to tea. "But you mustn't mind the muddle," she said. "We're still waiting for the men to finish the upstairs rooms. Matt had to sleep in the hall last night."

"Yes, he did really!" Jane said. "And tonight it's my turn, isn't it, Mummy?"

Mrs Lindsay said, smiling at Anna, "They fight over these privileges. Personally I prefer a bedroom! Jane, show her around. Tea's in the bear garden as usual." She picked up a pile of folded curtains. "I must just take these up."

Jane laughed at Anna's surprised face. "That's the name of our own room, I'll show you in a minute. Mummy, can we eat the doughnuts?"

"Yes, I've laid it all ready."

Anna was looking at a watercolour hanging on the wall at the foot of the stairs. It was a picture of the staithe and sailing boats on the creek.

"Gillie did that," said Jane, coming and standing beside her.

"Who's Gillie?" Anna asked in a low voice.

"She's a sort of pretend auntie – an old friend of Mummy's. Her real name's Miss Penelope Gill but we always call her Gillie."

"Don't you ever let her hear you calling her Penelope!" said Mrs Lindsay, laughing. "She hates the name, though really I can't see why. I suppose it wasn't so fashionable when she was young." She moved on up the stairs, then looked down over the banisters. "Are the others coming, Janey?"

"Yes, we shouted to them."

"Good." Mrs Lindsay smiled down at Anna. "Stay as long as you like. Do your people know you're here?"

Anna shook her head and mumbled shyly that it was all right, she didn't have to be back any special time.

"That's fine, then." Mrs Lindsay bent and picked up Roly who was following her up, step by step. "You come up with me, my love," she said, hugging him. "Jane, when you see the others coming, ring the bell, otherwise they may forget they're on the way home and start cockling or something!"

"Oh, yes!" Jane ran and fetched down a big cowbell from a shelf over the door. "Look, Anna, isn't it super? It came with the house. It's twice the size of an ordinary one. You can hear it halfway down the creek. Andrew tried it yesterday."

"You can hear it halfway down the creek"... For a moment Anna was convinced she had heard these words before somewhere. But where?... When...? Her mind went blank as she tried to remember.

Jane was at the window, peering down the creek, the bell in her hand. "Yes, there they are!" she cried.

She rang the bell, and Anna, watching from the narrow side window, saw the others – three specks of navy-blue in the distance – start running up the bed of the creek towards them.

Chapter Twenty-Six

SCILLA'S SECRET

FIVE MINUTES LATER they were all crowding into the long, low room known as the bear garden. Toys, books and games filled the shelves round the walls, and a long table running down the middle of the room was laid ready for tea.

Jane went to fetch the teapot and a large jug of milk from the kitchen, and Priscilla, running in just ahead of the boys, pulled out a chair for Anna and sat down quickly in the one beside her. She turned and smiled at Anna, her eyes shining.

Anna smiled back. "Did you find our note?"

"Yes, that's why I ran."

The others came in and they all started tucking in to the buns and doughnuts, while Jane poured out tea and milk. Everyone talked at once and everyone talked loudly. "Don't wait to be offered things," said Andrew. "Take what you want while it's there, otherwise you may miss it. But just to start you off, allow me to offer you a doughnut."

Priscilla said quietly to Anna, under cover of the general hubbub, "I hoped you'd come back. I've been wanting you to for ages."

"Have you?" Anna was pleased. "Why didn't you ask me?"

"I couldn't with the others there." Scilla glanced quickly round the table. "I saw you first, before any of them did. I saw you from my room." She lowered her voice and said softly and deliberately, "You know where my room is, don't you?"

Anna looked at her quickly. "Oh! Is it at the top, looking out over the creek?"

"Yes, the one at the end." Priscilla smiled a satisfied, secret smile, and buried her teeth in a slice of bread and jam. In a minute she said, still in the same low voice, "Did you mind when we caught you the other day? You looked a bit frightened at first and I thought perhaps we shouldn't have. I wanted to catch you by myself, without all the others. I thought it would be more fun, but of course Andrew got there first, *as* usual."

"What did Andrew do first *as* usual?" called Andrew from the other side of the table. "Stop whispering, you two. Do you know, Anna, Scilla thinks you're her own property, just because she made up a story about you before she ever saw you!"

"Did you?" Anna turned to her. "What sort of story?"

Priscilla smiled and said nothing.

"Has she told you her secret name for you yet?" asked Andrew.

"Yes, tell us!" said Jane. "What is it?"

Anna shook her head. "I don't know." She looked at Scilla hopefully, but Scilla was not saying any more. She sat quietly smiling to herself, looking as if she was in a contented daydream, but eating steadily all the while. Bun after bun disappeared into her mouth, apparently almost unnoticed. Anna was quite surprised. Priscilla was the least fat of all the Lindsays.

Anna herself was eating more than she usually did in other people's houses. This was the first time she could ever remember going out to tea and enjoying it. Mrs Lindsay not being there made it easier, but even when she came in once or twice, she accepted Anna so much as a matter of course that Anna could not help feeling at home.

After tea they all went into the kitchen to wash up. Anna was hanging around hopefully, trying to look helpful – although she had not the least idea where anything was kept – when Scilla came running to her and under pretence

198

of offering her a drying-up cloth, whispered something quickly in her ear.

Anna looked puzzled and bent her head lower.

Scilla whispered again. "I left it on the beach."

"What?" Anna was mystified.

"You – something I was doing for you. I thought you'd be staying on down there as usual, and would find it. It was pretty."

"I'll look for it tomorrow," said Anna.

"It won't be there, the tide will have washed it away." Scilla was looking at her expectantly. Anna thought quickly. The tide would still be out. If she ran down there soon she might still see whatever it was before she had to go back to the cottage. But she did not want to leave yet. Not so soon!

"Shall I go when I leave here?" she asked. Scilla nodded eagerly. "What is it?" Anna asked, smiling.

Scilla looked up at her from under her eyelashes, then said in a whisper, "Your secret name!"

She skipped away before there was a chance to ask her any more, and though several times during the next hour Anna caught Scilla looking at her with the same expression of quiet excitement – as if she were hugging some secret to herself but quite happy to wait until Anna was ready to share it – nothing more was said between them.

Anna stayed on until Matthew, and then Scilla had been sent up for their baths, and Mrs Lindsay had come in and was beginning to tidy up. Jane was upstairs singing to

Roly, who was now as wide awake as he had been sleepy an hour earlier. Anna helped Mrs Lindsay stack away the games on the shelves, while Andrew, yawning, sprawled on the window seat and gazed out over the water.

"There, that's fine!" Mrs Lindsay turned and smiled at Anna. "Time to go now," she said gently. "Look at poor old Andy nearly dropping off his perch! But do come again. Come whenever you feel like it, and thank you for helping to tidy up." She smiled again and went out of the room without waiting for a reply.

Anna followed uncertainly, suddenly tongue-tied, but saw, as she came out into the hall, that Mrs Lindsay was now busy in the kitchen. Through the half-open door she could see her, back view, as she stood arranging things on the larder shelves. She was singing to herself under her breath. Anna hesitated, wondering if she would come out again, then slipped thankfully out of the side door, closed it quietly behind her, and ran.

Never, never had she liked being in anyone else's house so much! Mrs Lindsay might almost have known that Anna's voice always failed her when it came to saying "thank you for having me". She had not even given her a chance to say a proper goodbye! It was almost as if, in leaving the formal goodbyes unsaid, she had left the door open behind Anna so that she really could come back whenever she felt like it.

She ran back to the cottage, cheeks flushed and eyes

shining, told a startled Mrs Pegg that she would not be long, and set off again down towards the sea.

The tide had already turned when she reached the beach. The sky had clouded over, and it looked grey and solitary, very different from the sunny place where they had played cricket that afternoon. It had been silly to come all this way just to see something written in the sand by a little girl, she thought. But she had wanted to come. She liked Scilla and was pleased at her wanting to share a secret with her, even if it was only a childish one.

She walked down to the water's edge, and saw it. Shells and strips of seaweed had been used to make a careful pattern of each letter, and the name MARNIE lay spelled out on the sand.

Chapter Twenty-Seven

HOW SCILLA KNEW

"BUT HOW DID you know?" Anna asked, still amazed. "What made you think of that name?"

It was the next morning, and she and Scilla were sitting on the wall at the top of the stone steps outside The Marsh House. Anna had hardly been able to wait to see Scilla again and ask her.

"Did you like it?" Scilla asked eagerly. "Did you think it was pretty?"

"Yes – yes, it was lovely. But how did you know?" Anna asked again.

"Well, I'll tell you. I wasn't sure at first – I kept wondering – and then when I asked you if you knew my room I was sure. I was almost sure before – but there are some things I just can't understand. I mean, well, look at this –" she leaned forward and pointed to a rusted iron ring that hung from the outside of the wall. "You see? It's broken – rusted away – how could you have tied the boat to that? And yet there isn't another anywhere. There isn't anything else you could have used. I've looked everywhere."

"I – I don't understand –" Anna was looking at her in bewilderment.

"I mean – if it was after dark – you know about going out in the boat in a nightie? – Well, what was the boat tied up to if that ring—"

Anna interrupted. "Scilla, tell me – *how* did you know?"

"It's in the book," she whispered.

"What book?"

Priscilla glanced round to make sure they were alone. "I found it in my room. The carpenter'd been taking down a cupboard in the wall – because I'm going to have a proper little built-in wardrobe – and this book was stuck in the back of the shelf. We came down here the very day he was doing it, and I was in my room when he pulled it out. So I kept it. It's my room, so it's my secret."

"What sort of a book is it?" Anna asked wonderingly.

"Just an old exercise book. It's got 'Marnie' written on the cover and inside it's a sort of diary. Lots of pages are torn out, there isn't an awful lot in it, but it was enough to give me an idea. That's how I knew who you were. Why do you call yourself Anna?"

"It's my name. Why – did you – did you think I was someone else?"

Scilla's face clouded. "Aren't you Marnie?" she whispered.

Anna shook her head confusedly. "No. No, but—"

Scilla stared at her blankly. "Then why did you come back? What are you doing here?" Her eyes filled suddenly with tears of angry disappointment. "I thought you were Marnie. I was sure you were." She looked so dejected now that Anna longed to comfort her, but her own thoughts were in a muddle and she found it difficult to think clearly.

"Anyway," Scilla said, "if it wasn't your own name why did you recognise it? You asked me how I knew!"

"Listen," Anna said slowly, "I don't think there is any such person as Marnie. I think she was a – a sort of imaginary girl that I—"

"That you what?"

"That I made up once – because I was lonely. I don't really remember now. It all seems a long while ago…" She sat staring down at the water which was beginning to lap at the foot of the stone steps. "I wish I could remember…" She turned to Scilla suddenly. "But you knew about her! That's exciting – that means we both shared the same imagination!"

Scilla leapt to her feet. "Wait! Wait here a minute and I'll show you." She ran back into the house.

In a moment she was back, apparently empty-handed, but holding something pressed tightly against her, inside her jersey. Her eyes were bright with excitement now.

"I don't want the others to see. Let's get down here." They moved down to a lower step and sat close together, almost out of sight of the house. For a moment Anna had the curious feeling that once, long ago, she had sat on the same step with someone else. Then she glanced sideways at Scilla, and the feeling disappeared.

"Here you are." Scilla drew the book out from under her jersey and laid it on Anna's lap. It was a limp, thin exercise book, creased and torn, with a faded grey-green cover. The name "Marnie" was written across the front. "Go on, read it," said Scilla.

Anna turned the pages and saw that it was half-filled with round, childish writing. She read a few lines.

I wish I had a friend here. The village children come on the staithe sometimes under my window and eat lickerice bootlaces and tell secrets. I wish I could go down and play with them.

"Now do you remember?" Scilla demanded, laughing up into her face. "You couldn't have written all that and really forgotten every word, could you? But it is fun sharing the same imagination! You invented her. And now, if you've forgotten her, I know more about her than you do! She was a funny sort of girl."

Anna stared at the book, turning it over in her hands. "But I didn't write it. Truly I never saw it before!"

"You didn't write it? But you must have. I expect you wrote it a long while ago, when you were much younger, and put it away in that cupboard and forgot all about it."

"But how would I get up there to put it in the cupboard?"

Scilla said, her mouth dropping open, "But didn't you live here?"

"No. Never." They stared at each other in amazement. "Why should you think I did?"

Scilla buried her head in her hands, running her fingers through her hair, then turned to Anna with an expression of puzzled astonishment. "But I *always* thought you did! Right from the beginning. Let me think now – the day we came down, that was the first time I saw you. We were getting out of the car and I saw you running out of the gate. I said to the others, "Look at that girl!" but they none of them saw you. Then we went in – and I told you – the carpenter was up in my room and he'd just pulled this book out from the back of the shelf. I didn't have time to read it but I just looked at it quickly, and I could see it belonged to someone who'd lived here before, so I hid it away. I read it after.

"Then I saw you again. You were always on the marsh or the beach by yourself and I thought, that girl looks like the girl in the book. She's always alone, playing tracking games on her own in the sandhills. But when I told the others they said I was inventing you—" she paused, running her hands through her hair in the same bewildered way.

"But I *knew*. I could tell by the way you kept looking up at the windows – mine especially. And yet the others never saw you! Well, then I noticed you hadn't got a boat of your own – and the girl in the book had – and I noticed about that ring being rusty, and things like that, and I began to wonder if you were a sort of ghost, and I thought perhaps that was why the others didn't see you.

"So I asked the carpenter one day. I said, 'Do you know a girl with dark hair who's very brown, and always goes about alone?' And he said yes, you'd been up here the day we came. I tried to find out why, but he didn't know. He just said you'd been asking about the people who used to live here. So then I was sure you were Marnie. I even thought you might have come back to try and find your book. But the man said your name was Anna. I couldn't make that out for ages, and then I thought it must be that you wanted to keep it a secret that you used to live here. So I didn't tell anyone about that. But—" she hesitated, "I still didn't know for sure whether you were real or a sort of phantom!"

Anna stared at her. "But this book is real! And I didn't write it. That means Marnie isn't a made-up person. *She wrote it!*"

Chapter Twenty-Eight

THE BOOK

THEY SAT AND pored over the book together. Priscilla knew most of it by heart but to Anna it was all new. And yet, as she read, it became familiar, like a story she had once heard and forgotten. Certain things came back into her mind quite clearly – things she had once known, or heard about, she could not be sure which…

May 30th
Decided to keep a diary – the word "dairy" had been crossed

out and "diary" written alongside – *as it's only for me it doesn't matter if it's untidy. Nothing happened today.*

May 31st
I wish I had a friend here. The village children come on the staithe sometimes under my window and eat lickerice bootlaces and tell secrets. I wish I could go down and play with them.

June 3rd
Such fun! I went for a row in my nightie last night. The tide was high and it was quite dark. I shall do it again. They were in the kitchen and never knew.

June 5th
Father and Mother came today. I'm so lucky! But Mother is going back on Monday when Father goes. I wish they'd take me too but the air is better here. But I'm terribly lucky. Lots of children are starving, and in Belgium the children are woken up in the night by the sound of the guns and fighting. I'm silly to mind Pluto.

Scilla looked up. "What a strange girl she is! What does she mean about Belgian children? And who's Pluto? It sounds like a cartoon film."

"It was a dog," said Anna slowly, "a big black dog. At least, that's what suddenly came into my mind. Perhaps they had one and she was frightened of it."

Scilla looked round at her in surprise. "Oh, yes, I believe

you're right! How clever of you! There's an old dog kennel, a huge one, out at the front. Matt found it under the trees."

They turned to the book again and read on.

June 8th
Nan brushed my hair a long while today because she found out I'd borrowed her shawl for the beggar girl. I forgot to put it back and Ettie found it in the boat. Silly old thing, why does she want a shawl anyway? Lily says it's because she has toothache and won't go to the dentist and she wrapps it round her face in the night.

"You see what I mean, though?" said Scilla. "What's lending a shawl to a beggar girl got to do with having your hair brushed? She must have been a funny girl."

June 10th
Nan is as cross as two sticks. She locked me in my room because of last night. She caught me tying up the boat when I was in my nightie so there won't be any more midnight rows for a bit.

June 12th
Miss Q isn't coming any more. She says her mother's ill but I think she's tired of teaching me. Read Ettie's comic. The Phantom in the Tower. It was very eerie.

July. Sunday
Today I went all along the beach. There were some families

*in the sandhills and I hid and watched them. They didn't
see me. They had hard-boiled eggs and strawberry jam
puffs. Lucky things!*

"I thought that was us," said Scilla, pointing to the page.
"We did have hard-boiled eggs one day, but not strawberry
jam puffs. But I was sure you'd written it about us." Anna
shook her head silently, still reading.

*Monday
I went to the beach again and played a tracking game. Nan
can't say I'm making a nuisance of myself and picking up with
straingers because I'm not. I only watch them. Today I lay so
still in the grass that a skylark came right down to its nest beside
me. I shall keep a book of nature notes if I can get another book.*

"You see?" said Scilla. "She's always doing that, going
down there by herself, never with anybody, just watching
other people. Well, that's how you were – always by
yourself. Are you surprised I thought it was you?"

*July 9th
Today the village children were under my window and they were
teasing a little boy with a funny name, Winterman or something. They
made him cry then one of them gave him a sherbet bag so he stopped
crying and eat it, but he ate the bag as well so then they started
teasing him again. He looked so funny but I felt rather sorry for him.*

July 11th
Edward came. He will stay ten days so now I have
company. But he's too old.

Thursday.
Went to the beach.

Friday.
We made a little house in the dunes with some planks that
were washed up on the beach. I thatched it with marram
grass. It was more fun than making sand houses and
gardens on my own.

Monday.
Went riding with Edward.

Tuesday.
Edward tried to make me talk to P today. He says I ought
to face up to what I'm frightened of. I did try but he was
horred and kept barking and jumping up.

"There," said Scilla, "P for Pluto, you were right! I'd
forgotten that bit." Anna nodded silently, her eyes still fixed
on the page. There was a gap, then the last entry, undated.

Edward wants to take me to the windmill. I'M NOT GOING.
I wish he'd stop teasing me about it.

Anna looked up and stared quietly out across the water. The windmill... that had been the end of the story... Or had it? If only she could remember! But she would say nothing to Scilla yet. She must try and work it out for herself.

But even as she was thinking, trying to arrange her memories in some sort of pattern, there seemed nothing to work out after all. She had thought she remembered something. While she was reading the book she had remembered something. But now, with her eyes no longer on the pages, and with Scilla beside her looking expectantly up into her face, her mind suddenly cleared. It was all quite simple. She had once invented a story about an imaginary girl called Marnie, and now by some strange coincidence it turned out that a girl with the same name had once lived in The Marsh House, and had written a diary there.

And yet she had this strange feeling that she had actually known her and talked to her... It was like trying to remember a dream. She could only remember it – in flashes – when she was not trying. For the moment her mind had gone blank.

She turned to Scilla, suddenly practical, and said in a matter of fact voice, "I didn't write it, and that's certain. And that means that someone called Marnie really did live here. I wonder who she was." She stood up. "Look, the tide's come in almost up to our feet! Shall we go in, and show it to your mother?"

Scilla hesitated. "It's been my secret," she said – her voice was regretful – "it's been my secret for so long—

Oh, all right. Yes, let's show her. But don't say anything about me thinking you were Marnie! They'd only tease me and it would turn into one of those awful family jokes that go on and on. I couldn't bear that."

Anna shook her head seriously. "No, we'll keep that bit secret. Let's just tell her how you found it."

Anna did want Mrs Lindsay to see the book. But more than that she wanted an excuse for going in again herself. Mrs Lindsay had said come again any time you like, but it would be easier to go in with Scilla, for some definite reason.

Mrs Lindsay was upstairs tidying the bedrooms. She greeted Anna as if she were an old friend. "Be a darling and fold this," she said, tossing a striped blanket over to her. "Matt will insist on having it but he never uses it, and I invariably find it rolled up in a ball under the bed."

Anna folded the blanket, proud to have been asked, and while Mrs Lindsay tidied the other bed, Scilla told her about the finding of Marnie's diary. "Look, here it is," she said, producing it from under her jersey. "Do read it, Mummy. Now."

Mrs Lindsay took it, glanced at it curiously, then sat down on Matthew's bed, and gave it her full attention.

"This really is rather interesting," she said slowly. "I believe it's quite old. I mean, not many children have nurses and governesses these days, do they?"

"Governesses?" said Scilla.

"Yes, here – Miss Q. 'I think she's tired of teaching me.' She will have been a governess, I imagine. Do you know, I can't help feeling this goes back quite a few years." She turned over a page. "Yes – look, this about the Belgian children! That refers to the First World War, I'm sure it does. When was that, now – 1914 to 1918?"

She looked up at the children, quite excited. "Do you know, I believe this book's about fifty years old! How clever of you to have found it!" She looked at Anna as well as Scilla, but Anna murmured that it was not she who had found it. "Oh, well, I expect you helped in some way," said Mrs Lindsay, apparently determined to include her. "Anyway, it seems to be the property of you two, whichever of you found it. I think it's fascinating."

She glanced back at the book. "Poor child, what a lonely life she seems to have led! I wonder who she was. Where did you say you found it? Come and show me now."

Scilla led the way across the landing, and Anna saw, for the first time, the little room that had once been Marnie's. It had been freshly papered and painted, and Scilla showed her with pride the built-in wardrobe that had taken the place of the old cupboard. Everything would have been changed since Marnie wrote her diary up there, but the view from the window must still be the same. Anna went over and looked out.

Below her was the staithe, narrowing every minute as the tide came in, then the creek, blue and shining in the morning sun, and beyond that the wide stretch of marsh laid out like a soft grey-green and mauve blanket. In the far distance she could see two small figures running and jumping over the streams, and although they were scarcely more than pin-head size, recognised them at once. "Oh, look, there are Andrew and Matthew!" she said, turning to the others.

Mrs Lindsay joined her at the window. "Yes, they went dabbing, and now I see they're on the way back," she said. "But they've left it too late, silly fellows. It looks as if they'll have to swim across the creek!" She paused, with her hands on the sill, gazing across the marsh to the sandhills and the sea beyond. "Isn't it wonderful how far you can see from here? That little girl must have spent hours up here, looking across the marsh. I shouldn't think she missed seeing anyone who ever went across it."

"Well, I don't either!" said Scilla. "That's how I first saw Anna. Or almost."

"And there's Wuntermenny!" said Anna, pointing to a small, humped-up figure sitting in the stern of what looked like a toy boat away up the creek.

"Who? Where?" asked Scilla, pushing up beside her at the window. "Do you mean that funny old fisherman who goes up and down in the boat?"

"*What* is his name?" asked Mrs Lindsay. "Did you say Winterman?"

"No, W—" Anna stopped with her mouth open. "Winterman – Wuntermenny – *that's* who the little boy was! The one who ate the sherbet bag – oh dear!" For a moment she hardly knew whether to laugh or cry. It was so exactly the sort of thing she would have expected Wuntermenny to do, and yet she had never before thought of his ever being a little boy! Oh, *poor* little Wuntermenny... She felt her eyes fill with sudden tears of sympathy, but brushed them away quickly before the others noticed.

"Of course!" Mrs Lindsay was saying, "That proves it. The book must have been written about fifty years ago – more, by the looks of that poor old fisherman, but you never can tell with some of these country people... I *must* ask Gillie when she comes. She'll probably know the answers to all these questions."

Chapter Twenty-Nine

TALKING ABOUT BOATS

"WHY SHOULD GILLIE know the answers?" asked Anna as she and Scilla went downstairs again.

"Because she used to come here when she was a child," said Scilla, "Didn't you know? Not to this house, but she might easily have known the people who lived here. It was she who told us it was for sale. Mummy'd written saying we were looking for somewhere near the sea, and she wrote back saying *do* go and look at The Marsh House. So they did, last Easter. And that's how we come to be here! You must meet Gillie when she comes. You'll like her."

"How did she know the house was for sale?" asked Anna.

"She still comes to Barnham sometimes. I expect that's how she heard about it. Isn't it fun, next time she comes she'll be coming to stay with us! That's why Mummy's so busy getting it ready. She wants her to come before the summer's over."

They had reached the side door and stood looking out on the shining water. On the far side of the creek Wuntermenny's boat was just putting in, and Andrew and Matthew were waiting hopefully at the water's edge.

"Good," said Anna, "he's going to ferry them across," and wished she had time to warn them that Wuntermenny hated being talked to. She looked at her watch. "I must go," she said regretfully, "I promised Mrs Pegg I'd do the vegetables."

"Oh, must you?" Scilla was disappointed. "The boys will be back in a minute. We might go somewhere, do something. Jane's only gone to the shop. Do come back!"

Anna did go back. She went back later that day, and again the next day, and every day, until Mrs Pegg said at last it was a wonder she didn't take up her bed and carry that round to The Marsh House too. But she winked at Sam as she said it, and it was clear she was pleased to see Anna so happy. Sam remarked contentedly that she was a good little biddy, and for all she might not be so mealy-mouthed, he'd a sight rather have her than that there Sandra-up-at-the-Corner. For his part he liked a lass with some go in her. And no-one could say Anna lacked that these days.

Some mornings she was up and dressed even before Mrs Pegg, and several times she turned up at The Marsh House even before the Lindsays had finished breakfast. She was surprised one morning to find a strange man sitting with them at table, and even more surprised to learn that this was Mr Lindsay. She had forgotten he would be coming down sometimes at the weekends. The Lindsays were surprised, too, to see Anna looking so suddenly shy.

"Goodness, I'd forgotten you didn't know Daddy!" said Jane. "Daddy, this is Anna."

"What!" said Matthew, looking at his father, "Do you mean to say you don't know Anna? She almost lives with us."

"Take no notice of him," said Andrew, "and don't look so scared, Anna. It's only Dad."

Mr Lindsay shook hands with Anna and said, smiling, "I'm not sure if it's me or Matt you're supposed to take no notice of, but I don't a bit mind if it's me. How do you do? Sit down and have some marmalade. Do you like it slippery or chunky?"

"Slippery, I think – usually," said Anna, still a little startled.

"Ah, I like it chunky." Mr Lindsay sat down again and

finished spreading himself a slice of bread and marmalade, then cutting a strip off the end he handed it to Anna. "Try that," he said gravely. "It's a rather super chunky, my wife made it. If you like it you can have some more; if not, spit it out when I'm not looking and help yourself to some slippery. It's up the other end. Do you mind awfully if I read the paper?"

"Oh, no."

Mr Lindsay returned behind the newspaper. Anna was relieved, but she liked him. He had been perfectly serious about the marmalade, and he was perfectly serious about not minding if he was not noticed. In fact he seemed to prefer it. She felt she knew where she stood with him.

"About the boat—" said Matthew.

"Oh yes!" said Scilla. "Tell Anna."

They all began telling her at once, explaining that they had been talking about getting a boat; they wanted one, they *needed* one. Marnie had had one, it had been tied to a ring in the wall – the Lindsays had all read the diary by now, and "Marnie" had become a familiar household name. The old ring was rusted away but they could easily fix a new one; all they needed was the boat to tie on to it. The question was what kind of boat.

"Dad thought a sailing boat," said Andrew, "and I agree. But Mum says a motor boat, and the girls just want some silly little pram they can row around in. What do you think?"

Anna knew nothing about boats – apart from Wuntermenny's – but she loved being included in a family conference like this, and it was only when Andrew had gone upstairs to fetch a catalogue, and the others had picked up their empty plates and drifted into the kitchen where Mrs Lindsay was already washing up, that she remembered Mr Lindsay was still there.

He looked round his paper suddenly. "Hello! Where have they all gone?"

"To wash up," said Anna.

"Ah, I thought they must have. The silence was deafening me. Did you spit it out, by the way?"

"Oh, the marmalade!" Anna laughed. "No, I liked it."

He nodded approvingly. "Have they been talking about getting a boat?"

"Yes."

"It's a funny thing," said Mr Lindsay, his eyes twinkling, "but they've got one already if they only knew it! Not that it would be much use to them... Have you discovered it yet?"

"No. Where?"

"Go and look along the hedge, past where the wall juts out on to the staithe. Go past the little shed and look in the hedge just beyond it. It's not much to look at, but it is rather interesting." He rose and folded his newspaper. "I must go and see to my books – forty million of them, all waiting to be read and sorted out. Goodbye – and good hunting!"

Anna went out. She went past the place where the wall jutted out, and along to where the hedge began, then, following it along on the inside, came to what must once have been the far end of the kitchen quarters. The little shed was there, set back against the hedge, and beyond that were disused cellars, outhouses, and a small cobbled yard which she had never seen before. On the farther side of the shed she began searching in the hedge, peering into the thick green leaves and pushing aside the twigs with her hands. And then she found it.

It was standing almost upright, cradled and supported by the hedge which had grown up all round it, and now almost entirely enclosed it – a small brown dinghy, old and rotten, its planking falling apart. Anna leaned forward, pushing her way into the hedge, and felt around inside. Her hand came up against something hard. An iron bar of some kind. She grasped it and pulled it towards her through the crackling twigs, forcing a way through them until they snapped. She drew out her hand, scratched and bleeding, and looked down to see what she had salvaged from this secret, hidden wreck.

It was a small anchor, rusted and blackened with age.

"Well, did you find anything?" asked Mr Lindsay, when they met again later in the day. The Lindsays were sitting on the terrace at tea-time, and as usual Anna was with them.

She nodded eagerly. "Oh, yes!" The others looked up curiously.

"And what did you think of it? Wasn't it interesting?"

"*Yes*!"

"Do they know yet? Have you told them?"

"Not yet." Anna was smiling.

"Hey, what's this?" cried Andrew. "What's the mystery?"

"Yes, tell us, Dad," said Matthew. "Tell us!" pleaded Jane and Priscilla.

"Shall we?" Mr Lindsay asked Anna. "Go ahead, then. Or better still, let's take them and show them."

They went along to the place where the boat was

hidden. Mr Lindsay separated the branches of the hedge and the children took it in turns to peer through.

"To think I missed it!" said Matthew, who was usually the first to find things. Andrew remarked knowledgeably that "she must have been quite a decent little craft at one time," and Jane was enchanted. Scilla gazed through the leaves with awestruck eyes. "Marnie's boat!" she murmured.

"Is there anything in it, do you think?" asked Matthew.

"Try and see," said his father. Matthew felt around and shook his head. Then Andrew tried. Then Mr Lindsay. There was nothing.

"Well, she must be pretty old if she really was Marnie's boat," said Andrew. "I don't know what we could have expected to find. I wonder how long she's been in that hedge."

Only Anna said nothing. No-one would know the anchor had been there. And no-one else could possibly want it. She hardly knew why she had wanted it so much herself, but from the moment when she had pulled it from the hedge and stood staring at it, she had known it was the one thing above all else that she wanted to keep for her own.

It was now hidden in a secret place. Anna had carried it there, rather curiously disguised, less than an hour after she had found it. Mrs Pegg would have been surprised if she had known the use to which her dirty-linen bag had been put.

Chapter Thirty

A LETTER FROM
MRS PRESTON

IT WAS A week later when the postman handed Anna a letter from Mrs Preston.

The sight of the familiar handwriting gave her a guilty pang. So much seemed to have happened during the past week or two that she had forgotten to send even a postcard home.

First there had been the finding of Marnie's boat. Then there had been the excitement over the new sailing dinghy which Mr Lindsay had now promised to buy. There had been a trip to Wells-next-the-Sea with the family, where they had all been fitted out with lifejackets, and had later eaten fish and chips, sitting on the edge of the quay with their legs dangling over the water.

It had seemed strange going into shops again. Anna had wandered round a big store with Jane and Scilla, quite amazed at the variety of things to be bought – and without which she had been perfectly happy all those weeks at Little Overton. Coming out of the shop, laughing with the others, she had run into none other than Sandra Stubbs, who had turned and stared at her with her mouth open. Anna, about to avoid her eye, had suddenly changed her mind and said, "Hello, Sandra!" just as if they were old friends, and Sandra, gaping, had replied with an astonished grunt.

Standing now by the Peggs' yard door, Anna looked down at the letter in her hand and felt her heart sink. She frowned, screwing up her eyes against the bright sunlight, and read:

Miss Hannay has called – rather distressed at not seeing you. She hadn't known you were away. She tells me I have done wrong, dear, in not telling you something before. (About money, Anna thought. I know it already.) *In any case I should like very much to see you again – there are things I want to tell you, dear – and it is easier talking than writing, I thought of coming down on Thursday next. There's a cheap*

*day trip that would get me to you by about 12.30. Let me
know on the enclosed card if it will be all right. All well at
Number 25. Raymond was home at the weekend. He sent his
love to you. So does Uncle. Looking forward to seeing you,
dear.*

  Your very loving Auntie.

Anna looked again at the extra "very" in the last sentence,
then pushed the letter in her pocket and set off for The
Marsh House, thinking as she went.

It would be silly for Mrs Preston to come all this way
just to tell her something she knew already. Should she
write and say she knew? – "Dear Auntie, I know about
the money. I've known for a long time, so you needn't
worry..." She felt a sudden spurt of anger against Miss
Hannay for having made Mrs Preston feel guilty. *She tells
me I have done wrong, dear* – what right had Miss Hannay
to tell Auntie she had done wrong? "Tell Miss Hannay to
mind her own business..."

No, it would be too difficult. Besides, it might look as
if Anna did not want to see her. And she did – partly – in
a way... It looked as if Auntie would have to come after
all. She turned the corner and ran along the footpath to The
Marsh House.

The Lindsays greeted her with their usual warmth,
full of their own domestic excitements. Everything was
wonderful. The boat had been definitely ordered, Dad

was coming down tonight, and this afternoon, as the tide would be low, they were all going cockling. Wasn't it a wonderful day! The weather forecast prophesied another heatwave. Best of all, Gillie was coming next week, and she was going to stay two whole days and nights. Mrs Lindsay had finished the spare-room curtains this morning, just before the letter came. Wasn't it lucky!

Anna, listening, felt her own small problems drifting away like the mist on the marsh.

"You'll like Gillie," said Jane.

"She painted the picture in the hall, you know," said Scilla.

"Yes, she's an artist," said Matthew. "And she knows all about Little Overton. She'll tell you about when the ships used to come right in to the staithe for loading, when her father was young."

"She's fairly old herself," said Jane.

"But she's a dear," said Mrs Lindsay. "You must be here when she comes, Anna." She turned to her with a smile. "What a terrible family we are for talking only about ourselves! And we haven't seen you since at least yesterday evening. Tell us what's new with you. Is that a letter sticking out of your pocket?"

"Yes, it's from my auntie." Anna hesitated. "I think she's coming down for the day."

"Oh, that will be nice! When is she coming?"

"On Thursday."

"On Thursday? Oh dear—" Mrs Lindsay looked thoughtful. "What a pity, that's the day our Gillie's coming. I would have liked to meet your auntie so much—"

"But Gillie isn't coming till after tea, Mummy," said Jane. "She said about six."

"So she did!" Mrs Lindsay turned to Anna again. "Do bring her round to see us. Do you think she would like to come to tea? It would have to be rather early, if Gillie's arriving at six."

"She'd have to leave early anyway," Anna said doubtfully. "She'd have to catch the five-thirty bus to the station."

Mrs Lindsay said, "Shall I write and ask her? Do you think she'd like to come?"

Anna considered, and thought she might.

For a moment she had found it impossible even to imagine Mrs Preston at The Marsh House, but the more she thought about it, the more she wanted her to come. She wanted her to see the Lindsays, and she wanted to see her *with* the Lindsays. If they liked her and she liked them, then – even if only for an hour – Anna's two worlds would be joined into one.

At the back of her mind, too, was a thought she had not yet allowed herself to think about seriously. Her holiday could not last for ever. It was already August, and although the subject had never actually been mentioned, she knew she would have to go home again before next term began. If, when she was back at home, she could talk about the

Lindsays, and Auntie knew the people she was talking about, it would make all the difference. Yes, she *must* come.

It was all arranged. Mrs Lindsay would write to Mrs Preston separately. And Anna wrote her card, adding casually, as if it were an afterthought, *by the way, we've been asked out to tea. She's writing to you.*

Chapter Thirty-One

MRS PRESTON GOES
OUT TO TEA

BY THE TIME Thursday came, Anna was not so sure she had done right to accept the invitation. Suppose Mrs Preston was in one of her worrying moods, or wore the brown hat that Anna always hated? She watched anxiously for the bus and was relieved beyond measure when Mrs Preston stepped down wearing a new straw hat that she had not seen before.

"Oh, Auntie, what a pretty hat!"

"Do you like it? Will it do?" Mrs Preston was

obviously relieved too. "You must tell me, dear – in a minute, when I've said hello to the others – who *are* these people? I had such a nice letter. – Ah, there you are, Susan! And Sam! How are you both?"

Mrs Preston was told all about the Lindsays over lunch. Anna was surprised to learn that Mrs Pegg seemed to know as much, or even more about them than she knew herself. Apparently Miss Manders at the Post Office knew all about them, too. They were extremely nice people. London people, but not the kind who made themselves unpopular in the village. He was a scholar, a very clever man. The quiet type. She was charming. The children were all charming too. If they hadn't been, Mrs Pegg would not, of course, have let Anna be always round there – that went without saying. As it was, it had been nice for the little lass to have company. And wasn't she looking all the better for it?

Mrs Preston agreed that she certainly was, and said she was looking forward to meeting Mrs Lindsay and thanking her for her kindness to Anna.

Nevertheless, as the time drew near she grew increasingly nervous.

"I had things I wanted to talk to you about," she said to Anna as they went upstairs to get ready. "But I think perhaps this isn't quite the moment. Perhaps if we can get away early—?"

"Yes," Anna said uneasily.

"We might go for a little walk, perhaps – just you and I?"

"Yes."

Mrs Preston looked at her reflection in the mirror, and pushed some loose strands of hair under her hat with trembling fingers. Then she turned and faced Anna with her head on one side. "Will I do, dear?"

Anna made a little move towards her. "Yes, of course. You're fine." She stopped awkwardly. If only she wouldn't look so *anxious* all the time! She thought of Mrs Lindsay's easy, friendly manner. "You're fine. There's no need to worry. And you needn't say good afternoon or how do you do, or anything like that when we get there." She tried to make her voice sound casual and off-hand. "I mean hello is quite good enough. That's all Mrs Lindsay ever says."

Mrs Preston looked quite alarmed. "But, dear, I always say how do you do! It would seem so strange, so rude…"

Anna frowned. Whatever she said was only going to increase Mrs Preston's anxiety. Perhaps she had better not mention the bear garden, and that it would not be a polite afternoon tea, anyway. That might put her off still more. She touched her on the arm awkwardly. "It'll be all right. Whatever you do."

"Well – I do hope so…" Mrs Preston was more doubtful than ever but she smiled gratefully. "Hadn't we better go now, dear? She did say half past three, didn't she?"

"Yes, but that doesn't matter. I mean they're not a bit

fussy about time. There isn't any hurry. It doesn't really matter *what* time we get there." Anna moved towards the door with a desperate attempt to appear casual. "Still, I suppose we may as well—"

They set off.

Mrs Lindsay opened the door herself. She had changed her usual thick jersey and slacks for a jumper and skirt, and greeted them with a warm, welcoming smile.

"How do you do?" she said, holding out her hand to Mrs Preston. "I'm so very glad you were able to come. Do come in. Hello, Anna. What, you again!"

Anna grinned sheepishly, and Mrs Preston, with a startled apologetic glance at Anna, shook hands with Mrs Lindsay.

"I thought we'd have tea in here, it's more comfortable," said Mrs Lindsay, leading the way towards the drawing-room. "Anna can go in the bear garden with the others if she'd rather, but it'll be a treat for me to be more civilised for a change."

There was a sudden clatter on the stairs, and two steel tubes of a vacuum cleaner came hurtling down, followed by Matthew, then Andrew, Jane and Priscilla. They drew up short with expressions of horror at seeing Mrs Preston.

"Here, what's going on?" Mrs Lindsay brushed aside Matthew's laboured explanation that it was the quickest way of bringing them down and that *she* had forgotten them, and said, "Come and say how do you do to Mrs

Preston, all of you. Oh, Roly-poly, what *have* you been up to?" – as Roly emerged from the drawing-room on all fours, his face streaked with jam. "Jane, be a darling and take him to the kitchen for a clean-up – no, perhaps I'd better." She picked him up under one arm and turned to Mrs Preston. "I'm so sorry, I shan't be a tick. No, don't worry, it's only jam."

She disappeared into the kitchen. Anna collected the vacuum-cleaner tubes, and the Lindsay children shook hands with Mrs Preston.

"We've been rushing about tidying up all day," said Matthew, looking up at Mrs Preston with interest. "Not only for you," he added thoughtfully, "but for someone else we've got coming as well."

"No, it *was* for you," Jane put in hastily with a reproving glance at Matthew.

"Yes, well partly, anyway," said Matthew, "but I mean you're not sleeping here, are you?" Mrs Preston looked bewildered. "Anyway I hope you think it looks better. By gum, we did have a rush round!"

"Don't be silly," said Andrew. "She didn't see it before, so how could she see the difference now?"

"I think it looks very nice," said Mrs Preston, her eyes flicking nervously round the hall. "A charming house, isn't it, Anna?" Anna nodded in dumb misery.

"Anyway, you should have seen it this morning!" said Matthew. "And a few weeks ago it was worse. When my

bed was over there—" he pointed to the corner of the hall
– "Andrew forgot one night and fell over it in the dark
with a bucket full of dabs. Phew! We couldn't get rid of
the pong for ages—"

"Did you have a pleasant journey?" Jane asked quickly.

Mrs Preston looked relieved. "Yes – oh, yes, thank
you. It was very nice, very pleasant. I think it's so kind of
your mother to invite me."

"Oh no, not at all!" said Jane.

"We *wanted* to see you," said Scilla.

"Yes, we couldn't imagine what you'd be like," said
Matthew. Andrew kicked him, and he looked round in
surprise.

"And now you know," said Mrs Preston, laughing
nervously. She touched the back of her hat and gave
Anna a rather desperate glance.

"Yes," said Matthew. But Anna saw, to her relief, that
he was still wearing his friendly grin.

Mrs Lindsay came hurrying back. "I'm so sorry," she
said. "Jane, you take Roly, will you? Now off you go, all
of you. We're going to have a quiet tea on our own. No
need to look so disappointed, Matt. You've got the same
as we have."

"Meringues?" he whispered, grinning.

Mrs Lindsay nodded. "Yes, go along with you!"

Matthew ran, and the others followed. From the
drawing-room Anna heard Mrs Preston say, "Five! How

lucky you are!" and Mrs Lindsay reply, "You're pretty lucky too. She's a darling, we're all—" then the drawing-room door closed.

She followed the others into the bear garden feeling quite dazed with surprise and relief.

Chapter Thirty-Two

A CONFESSION

"YOU HARDLY SAW the children did you?" said Anna, as she and Mrs Preston walked to the bus stop later.

"No, I didn't, did I?" Mrs Preston seemed vague and a little upset.

Anna glanced at her sideways, waiting for her to make some remark about the Lindsays without having to be prompted, but after a moment's silence she could bear the suspense no longer. "It was a pity you had to be in the drawing-room most of the time," she said. "You

239

might have liked it better with us. But she's awfully nice."

Mrs Preston looked round in surprise. "Who, Mrs Lindsay? Oh yes, dear, I thought she was a *very* nice woman. And she spoke so nicely about you. The children seemed nice too. Which was the one you said you particularly liked?"

"I *told* you—" Anna sighed. "Auntie, what is it? Did you hate it?"

"No, no, no! It's not that." Mrs Preston cleared her throat as if she were about to make a prepared speech, then she said, "I told you I wanted to talk to you, dear. I'm afraid I haven't confided in you as much as I should. Miss Hannay says I should have told you before – in fact she even seemed to think you might know already – the fact is, the council send us a cheque every fortnight to help with your expenses. It is only a contribution, you understand, and it's quite a normal procedure. But I want you to know it isn't that Uncle and I wouldn't pay for you ourselves – though I must admit it's been a help – but I realise now I should have told you before." She paused for breath, then added regretfully, "I always hoped you might never need know."

"Why?" asked Anna.

"I suppose I was afraid you might think we didn't love you enough. But even if we hadn't had the cheque it wouldn't have made any difference. You *do* believe that, don't you?"

A Confession

Anna felt a great load lift off her mind. "I wish you'd told me before," she said.

"I know, I should have. And now Mrs Lindsay says I should have told you more about your background. Not that I know very much, but even what little I knew I tried to forget—" she shook her head in a helpless sort of way and nearly stumbled, then pulled herself together again. "But I *did* try. I tried to tell you about your people – your mother, and your grandmother, but you never would listen. You always turned away as if you weren't interested."

I know, thought Anna. I hated them – and wondered why. After all, it was not their fault if they had died. She realised suddenly that the old hate had disappeared. It was as if, at some time – some time when she had not even been thinking about it – she had forgiven them all.

"But perhaps I didn't try as much as I should have," Mrs Preston went on. "You see, I wanted so much to feel you were my own daughter. I always hoped we might come to be friends—"

"Oh, Auntie, let's!" Anna slipped an arm through hers, finding for the first time that she was tall enough. "I know I've been ghastly and I expect I shall be again, but I do love you."

Mrs Preston patted the hand that was now so near hers and said, a little shakily, "I love you too, dear. I always have ever since you were a little thing." She drew herself up and wiped her eyes. "How tall you've grown! I'm beginning to feel quite a shrimp beside you!"

"Tell me what you were talking to Mrs Lindsay about all that time," said Anna, altering her pace to keep in step.

Mrs Preston smiled. "Quite a number of things. In fact my head's in a whirl. One thing I think may please you very much. She asked me whether I would let you stay on down here with them, as their guest, until they go back to London. Would you like that?"

"Oh, I should *love* it! Oh, Auntie—!" Anna almost hugged her. She was feeling extraordinarily happy.

They had arrived at the bus stop. Mrs Preston looked at her watch. "There was something else—" she said, glancing anxiously down the road to see if the bus was coming.

"Is it about my background?" said Anna suddenly.

"Yes. Yes, it is, dear. Though I'm afraid there isn't much I can tell you—" She broke off as the bus appeared round the corner. "There isn't time now," she said hurriedly. "Ask Mrs Lindsay. She'll tell you later. We had a long talk." She kissed Anna and looked at her with sudden pride. "She said such nice things about you."

"Did she – what?"

"Oh, that you were so honest and straightforward, and always so helpful. I felt quite proud." The bus drew up alongside. "Goodbye, dear. I wish it had been longer. I'll write."

She climbed up on to the step. Then, as the driver was still talking to a man inside, she beckoned to Anna to come nearer. "Uncle's been busy in your room," she murmured, "making a little surprise! I oughtn't to tell you really, but he's been papering and painting, and we've got a few things for it. It looks ever so pretty!" She nodded and smiled, with her finger to her lips, and the bus moved off.

Anna waved until it was out of sight, then turned thoughtfully away. Scilla was waiting at the corner of the road. She saw Anna coming and rushed to meet her.

"Did she tell you that you're coming to stay with us? Isn't it super? Mummy says you can come as soon as Gillie goes. Are you glad?"

"Yes, terribly glad!"

"Wasn't it a wonderful idea of Mummy's! Are you coming back now?"

Anna hesitated. "Is your mother very busy?"

Scilla laughed. "You should see her! You should see all of us. Mummy's cooking and rushing around, Jane's putting flowers and things in Gillie's room, Matthew's washing up, and Andy's trying to bath Roly-poly! I shall have to go back and help in a minute, but I *had* to come and find out if she'd told you. Mummy says she's awfully glad your auntie came, and she thinks she's a very nice woman – just in case you were wondering. Are you coming back? Mummy said if not, I was to ask you to come later, about half past seven."

Anna nodded. "I'll come later. I've got something I must do first."

They parted at the corner of the road and she walked slowly back to the cottage, thinking about the thing she had to do. She must write to Mrs Preston, straight away before she changed her mind.

It was only a short letter. *Dear Auntie, I couldn't tell you just now because the bus was coming but you said Mrs L said I was honest. Well, I'm not. I took some money out of your purse last term. It was mostly pennies but once there was a shilling. I put the shilling back but not all the pennies. I will pay you back when I come home, and I'm sorry. With tons of love.*

She underlined the "tons", signed her name, and stuck down the envelope with a sigh of relief. Then she went out to post it.

It was three hours later, but Anna had still not gone back to The Marsh House.

She was away out on the dyke, watching the wild geese flying across the sunset over the marsh, and hearing the strange honk-honking noise they made as they passed overhead. She turned and saw the first blue of twilight coming down over the distant village, and started back towards it.

As she came nearer The Marsh House she quickened her pace. She was late. Scilla was waiting for her, the Lindsays were all expecting her, and Gillie – Miss Penelope Gill, whom she had never seen – was probably expecting her too. But she could not have hurried before. She came to the corner, drew a deep breath, and ran along the footpath towards the house.

Mrs Lindsay was just coming out to look for her.

"Anna! What is it, dear? Where have you been? We've been waiting—"

"Where is Mr Lindsay? Can I see him first? I want to tell him something."

Mrs Lindsay looked surprised. "But he's gone. Didn't you know? He had to go back to town, to work. He won't be back until tomorrow night. What is it? Can I help?"

"I want to tell him something," Anna gabbled quickly, "something about the boat – Marnie's boat. It's something I took."

Mrs Lindsay put an arm round her shoulders and drew her into the hall. "Was it the anchor?" she asked casually.

Anna spun round. "How did you know?"

"He told me. Don't look so angry. There's nothing to be frightened of."

"You mean he knew it was there?"

Mrs Lindsay nodded. "Yes, of course. And he realised you must have taken it, because it wasn't there when you all went to look. It didn't matter a bit. He thought you'd probably tell him, because he knew you weren't the sort of person who just took things without asking. But when you didn't, he said you must have wanted it an awful lot, not to risk asking for it. *Did* you want it all that much?"

Anna nodded silently.

Mrs Lindsay said "O-oh," very gently, just as if Anna had hurt herself and was trying not to cry. "And you wanted to see him to tell him you'd taken it? You *are* a sweetie. I

245

call that jolly brave. Don't worry about it, of *course* you can have it. Tell me – where is it now?"

"Under my bed," Anna whispered. "In a suitcase."

Mrs Lindsay said "O-oh" again. "And what were you going to do with it – or isn't that a fair question?"

Anna hesitated, then said, "Yes, of course it's fair. I was going to – I thought perhaps, if I cleaned it up, I might – take it home and Auntie might let me hang it up in my room – for a – a sort of decoration." She gave a little gasp that was half a sob, half a giggle. "It sounds so feeble now but—"

Mrs Lindsay interrupted. "No, it's not feeble at all. Guess what my husband said to me before he left! He said, if I knew for sure she wanted it, I could have rubbed it down and given it a coat of silver paint. She could have had it to hang up on her wall."

Anna was amazed. "Did he truly say that?"

"Yes, truly. So bring it back some time and we'll hold him to it! Now, come in, darling, and meet Gillie. She's been longing to see you."

She bent down and kissed Anna, smoothing the hair away from her eyes, then, with an arm still round her shoulders, she pushed open the drawing-room door and they went in.

Chapter Thirty-Three

MISS PENELOPE GILL

AT FIRST ANNA thought Gillie was not there after all. Then she saw that the others were gathered round a little woman who was sitting in a low easy chair. Could this be Miss Penelope Gill? She had imagined her tall and thin and rather elegant, with straight dark hair cut in a fringe. This woman was small and dumpy, with short, shaggy grey hair.

She turned round as they came in, and Anna had her second surprise.

"So *you're* Anna!" said the little woman. "Why, we've met before, haven't we? What a blessing, we can do away with all those tiresome introductions and things! Do you know, I always wished I'd asked you what your name was. And now I know! I'm Gillie, by the way, but I expect you've guessed that already." She was looking at Anna was a long, steady gaze, as if she wanted to know everything about her, but her eyes were kind. "Do you remember me?" she asked.

Anna smiled. "Yes, you were painting on the marsh." She would have liked to add that she had remembered her ever since as if they had been friends, but felt this would be too extravagant.

The Lindsays were delighted and amazed, wanting to know how and when the two could possibly have met. And why hadn't they been there, they demanded. Miss Gill told them. It was the last time she had come down to Barnham for a few days' sketching.

She looked up at Anna. "We talked about this house, didn't we? And now we meet inside it! How very right and proper that seems. Sit down and tell me what you've been doing since we last met."

While everyone talked, Mrs Lindsay fetched a jug of hot cocoa and a pot of coffee from the kitchen. Jane brought in a tray of mugs and cups and saucers, and Matthew went round with the big biscuit tin. "We're staying up late tonight," he said with a grin, "so that we can eat biscuits while Gillie tells us one of her stories."

Miss Gill laughed. "Who said I was going to tell one of my stories, you saucy boy?"

"But you *always* do," said Matthew, looking surprised.

"Yes, she does," said Scilla, sitting down on the floor beside Anna. "And I've been longing for you to come! Isn't it fun – do you feel as if you're living here already?"

"I had a friend who used to live here once," said Miss Gill, smiling down at the two of them. "But I certainly never came to stay with her. In fact I doubt if I ever came right inside more than once."

"Why not?" asked Matthew.

Mrs Lindsay stopped pouring out the cocoa and looked round. "*Did* you?" she said. "In this house?"

Miss Gill said, answering them both at once. "Yes, dear, I'm sure I told you – or didn't I? Because they had a fierce dog, Matt. At least I always thought he was fierce. I know I was scared to death of him, so after that one visit I always met her outside if I could. Her mother and my mother were friends."

"What was her name?" asked Anna and Scilla both together.

"Marian," said Miss Gill.

Mrs Lindsay said quickly, "Gillie, we *must* show you our book. The children found it. We've been longing to ask you if you know anything about it – that's why we're all so interested. Where is it, Scilla?"

Scilla brought it out at once. She had been sitting with it tucked inside her jersey, only waiting for Anna to come before producing it. Now she laid it in Gillie's lap.

"What's this?" Gillie put on her spectacles. "Marnie?" she said slowly, reading the name on the cover. "But how did you know? Marian *was* always called Marnie –"

"We didn't know," said Mrs Lindsay, looking as excited as the children. "We found it here."

"It was stuck behind a shelf," said Scilla. "In *my* room." She glanced at Anna, smiling and hugging her knees.

Gillie opened the book and looked through it. Now and again little sighs and chuckles escaped her. Anna and the Lindsays waited, watching her face. Yes, it was Marian's book without a doubt. How strange – how extraordinary to come across it after all these years! She turned to the beginning again and read it through more slowly.

"Oh, those lucky children with their licquorice bootlaces!" she exclaimed. "How we used to envy them! At least, I know I did. It was during the Great War, you know, and sugar was in short supply. We were never allowed those rubbishy sweets, as my mother used to call them; only a few of the more wholesome kind, and precious few of those."

She turned the page. "And Pluto. Yes, that was the name of that dreadful dog! Perhaps he wasn't so fierce really… But apparently Marnie was afraid of him, too – fancy that, she never told me—! I don't know why they kept him but I think her father thought he would be good as a house dog, for when he was away…. Poor man, he was drowned shortly afterwards."

"Drowned?" said Matthew, in a shocked voice.

"Yes, in the war. He was in the Navy, you know."

"We didn't know—" Mrs Lindsay began, but Gillie was engrossed in the book again.

"And Miss Q! That was Miss Quick! What a dance we led the poor lady! She was the governess we shared – not together but on different days. She came to us two or three days a week, and to Marnie on the other days. I remember my brothers used to tease the poor woman dreadfully." She laid the book down and wiped her eyes. "Dear me, how it does take one back! This really is a most exciting discovery."

It was growing dark in the room. Mrs Lindsay went to turn on the light, then changed her mind and brought down two branched candlesticks instead. "Do go on, Gillie," she said. "It's fascinating to us, too. We don't know anything about the family except what you've just told us."

Gillie turned in her chair and said with a laugh, "I can see by the way you're lighting those candles, that you think I'm going to launch out on one of my long yarns. Well, perhaps I am. But you must stop me if you get bored."

"We shan't be bored," said Scilla, drawing closer to her. "We want to hear the story of Marnie."

"Very well," said Gillie. "Now, where shall I begin?"

Mrs Lindsay drew up her chair behind Anna, who was still sitting on the floor, and signed to her that she could lean back if she liked.

Anna turned and smiled, hesitated, then leaned back
– a little awkwardly at first, then relaxing gradually into
comfort. The candlelight made a soft glow in the room.
Outside, the darkening sky had turned to a deep blue, and
beyond the sound of Gillie's voice Anna could hear the
murmur of the returning tide.

Chapter Thirty-Four

GILLIE TELLS A STORY

"I DIDN'T REALLY know Marnie very well in those days," Gillie said. "We were a large family, not very well off, and we lived over beyond Barnham. We had no car then, so I didn't see her often, but we used to play together when my mother brought me to Little Overton. She was always very lively – marvellous company – and she always seemed thrilled at having me to play with. That used to surprise me rather, because I wasn't a particularly thrilling child, I can assure you! I was rather dull and stodgy. But I don't think she had many other friends."

"Why not?" asked Scilla.

"It was different in those days," Gillie explained. "Children didn't just make friends with each other casually, the way they do now," she said. "We always had to ask our mothers first."

"Goodness!" said Jane.

"Yes." Gillie smiled. "Marnie's mother was away a lot. She was young, and merry, and pretty, and she entertained a great deal at their house in London. Marnie always stayed with her nurse at The Marsh House all the summer."

"Jolly nice for her too," said Andrew, who was stretched out on the window seat behind them, pretending to be only half interested.

"Yes, indeed," said Gillie. "She was a lucky child in some ways. And I think she knew it. She thought the world of her parents. She was always boasting about them. It used to make me quite tired sometimes. After all, I much preferred my own, even if they weren't quite so rich or handsome or wonderful."

"She wasn't lucky at all," said Anna suddenly. "She had a beastly time. Most of the time anyway."

The others looked up, surprised. "You talk as if you knew her yourself!" said Andrew, laughing.

"Well, it's in the diary, isn't it? You said yourself she must have been jolly lonely," Anna turned to Mrs Lindsay.

"Yes, I did. That's true," said Mrs Lindsay.

"And you're quite right," Gillie said to Anna. "She did have a beastly time, but I didn't know it in those days.

I suppose in some ways she was a lucky child, living in this lovely house and staying by the sea all the summer, but it was only later I learned how unhappy she was. I was telling you how it seemed to me then."

Anna nodded and leaned back again.

"I must say, her mother never seemed to me quite like a proper mother – not like my own was – but she was very pretty," Gillie went on. "Marnie herself was a lively little monkey. This in the book, about her going out in the boat at night when they thought she was in bed… I'm sure I remember hearing about that. Miss Quick told my mother she was a naughty little thing – used to run quite wild sometimes. There was a story that she once brought a beggar girl in to one of her parents' smart parties" – her eyes twinkled – "I wish I could remember what happened exactly. I believe they pretended she was selling something – clothes pegs, perhaps."

Anna sat up suddenly. "Was it sea lavender?" she asked.

Gillie looked down at her in surprise. "Sea lavender, so it was! What ever made you think of that?"

"Yes, what made you?" said Scilla. "You couldn't have known. It isn't in the book."

Anna shook her head. "I don't know. It just came into my head all of a sudden that it was sea lavender – in little bunches."

"Magical Anna!" said Andrew.

"Yes, but it was rather odd," said Gillie. "Marnie was always so fond of sea lavender – I hadn't told you that, had I? – but they wouldn't let her bring it into the house because they said it dropped and collected the dust."

"Who were 'they'?" asked Jane.

"The two maids, and her nurse. My mother used to say it was a shame the way she was always left to the maids. I don't remember ever seeing them myself, but that nurse was a beastly woman from all accounts."

"Tell us! Tell us!" said the children.

"Goodness me," said Gillie, "how eager you all look to hear a tale of cruelty in the olden days! I'm afraid it's not a very dramatic tale either. But I remember my mother telling me, when it all came out afterwards. Apparently the nurse had been treating Marnie very badly while her parents were away, and the maids had been frightening her with silly stories. In fact she was quite neglected, though you'd never have guessed it. Certainly I never did."

"Why didn't she tell?" asked Scilla.

"She daren't. They'd threatened her with all sorts of silly things – one was that they'd shut her up in the windmill if she did. That's why she was so afraid of it." She pointed to the book lying open on her lap. "You see here, 'Edward wants me to go to the windmill but *I'm not going*.' "

"Oh yes, tell us about Edward!" said Matthew. "Who was he?"

"He was a distant cousin of hers. I don't think I ever met him in those days. But of course she married him later, so I did meet him then, once."

Jane was delighted. "There you are!" she said with a triumphant smile at her mother, "I said I bet she married Edward when she grew up. Was he nice?"

"Oh yes, I think so. I'm sure he was very kind to her. Though perhaps he was a little – well, a little severe. You've seen here, in the diary, where she says 'Edward says I ought to face up to things... I wish he'd stop teasing me' and so on. I think perhaps even then he was a little hard on her, without meaning to be."

She looked again at the last entry. "The windmill – that was the cause of all the trouble... Still, I suppose it was just as well, as it turned out."

"What was just as well? What happened?" Scilla demanded eagerly.

Gillie wrinkled her forehead. "That's the trouble, I don't really know what happened. I don't think anybody ever did, and I only heard the tale second-hand from my mother. But apparently Marnie was missing one night – when her parents were away – and the maids got into a panic and got some of the local men to make a search party. But it was Edward himself who found her; so then I think they wished they'd kept it to themselves! He said he'd found her lying on the floor at the top of the ladder in the mill, and he carried her down himself, and met the search party just coming along. My mother heard that bit of the story from her maid, so it may have been just local gossip. But anyway it all came out after that."

"What came out?" asked Anna.

"About her nurse bullying her, and not looking after her properly. But Marnie had never told a soul – that was the dreadful thing – so it didn't come out straight away even then. They punished her by locking her up in her room. And her parents were told she'd been running away with Edward and staying all night in the mill. I suppose the nurse was frightened by then (since half the village knew the child had been lost), and was trying to save her own skin. But it didn't work, I'm happy to say. Marnie was sent away to boarding school after that, almost immediately, and the nurse was sent packing. Wretched woman that she was."

They were all silent for a moment. Then Jane said in a puzzled voice, "But why did she go to the mill if she was so afraid of it?"

"My mother always said it was just naughtiness," said Gillie.

"But that doesn't make sense," said Jane. "You don't go somewhere you're frightened of just for the sake of being naughty."

Scilla said thoughtfully, "It says in the diary about making sand houses, and making a little house in the dunes with a thatched roof. I wonder if she and Edward were going to make it into a secret house of their own – if she'd stopped being frightened of it, perhaps—?"

Matthew interrupted. "*I* think she did it to give them all a scare. I hope she did, and serve them right."

"No," said Anna. "I think she went there just because she *was* frightened. To make herself not, I mean."

Gillie looked at her with interest. "I believe you're right, Anna. I never thought of it before, but it's just the sort of thing she might have done – if she'd been driven to it. Marnie always said she couldn't stand people going on and on at her about what she *ought* to do – that's why she couldn't bear Miss Quick. But with Edward it would have been different, she minded what he thought, and if he'd been teasing her…"

She sighed and leaned back in her chair, looking suddenly tired. "Poor Marnie," she said, almost under her breath. "It was all so long ago. And it seems so sad – now, looking back."

Chapter Thirty-Five

WHOSE FAULT WAS IT?

MRS LINDSAY JUMPED to her feet. "What a shame, Gillie, we're keeping you up and you're tired after your journey!" She made a move to collect the cups and saucers, but Gillie was almost out of her chair immediately.

"No, no, no!" she cried. "I *won't* go to bed yet. I'm not in the least tired. Nor are any of your young, by the looks of them. Sit down, there's a dear thing. Don't spoil a nice party just because a silly old woman starts reminiscing."

The others joined in with shouts of "Sit down, Mummy." "*You* go to bed." "Don't spoil everything!" and Mrs Lindsay sank quickly back in her chair. Gillie nodded approvingly.

"We want to hear more about Marnie," said Scilla.

"Tell us what happened afterwards," said Jane.

Gillie looked at Mrs Lindsay, who nodded back. "I'm as fascinated as they are," she said, smiling. "If anyone's bored they can always go away." She leaned forward suddenly to look at Anna, who was sitting with her head bent forward, almost as if she was dozing. "Are you awake, my love? You're supposed to be going back to the Peggs tonight, you know. Unless—" she broke off. "Andy, be a dear, run and ask Mrs Pegg if Anna can stay here for tonight. Tell her we've got everything she might want, and say I promise to send her back tomorrow. Will you?"

There were shouts of delight from the children, and Andrew leapt to his feet. Anna looked up with startled pleasure. "Can I? Really?"

Mrs Lindsay nodded. "Were you asleep?"

"No. I was wondering something—" Anna paused as the door closed behind Andrew, then said, looking across at Gillie, "I was thinking about when Marnie was in the mill. There wasn't anyone else there with her, was there?"

"Before Edward came? Oh no, I'm sure not."

"But suppose there had been – suppose someone else had been with her, would she have left them there?"

Gillie looked puzzled. "What an odd question, my dear. I don't quite see what you mean."

Anna insisted. "Suppose someone else *had* been with her, would she have gone away with Edward and left them alone up there – in the dark?" She kept her eyes fixed on Gillie, ignoring everyone else, only knowing that it was one of those questions that *must* have an answer, even if it sounded like nonsense.

Gillie saw that she was in earnest and thought seriously. Then she said, "If she had been conscious I'm sure she wouldn't – though fear can make people do terrible things sometimes. But in this case there was no question of it. Marnie was alone, and she was quite unconscious when they found her. I remember being told she never woke up until after they got her home and into bed. Poor child, I should think she was exhausted with fear." She gave Anna a steady, friendly gaze and said, "Does that answer your question?"

"Yes, I think so," said Anna, smiling back; and knew that she felt satisfied.

Scilla was waiting impatiently to hear the rest of the story. "Funny old Anna," she said, patting her foot affectionately, "don't go asking any more questions till we've finished hearing what happened. Go on, Gillie, tell us about when she grew up." She stopped, her eyes widening. "Where is Marnie now? If she was about the same age as you – I mean, you're not *that* old—"

The grown-ups laughed and Gillie said she now felt half as young again. Then she said, more seriously, "No, I thought I'd told you, Marnie died several years ago. But I'd rather lost touch with her some years before that. There isn't really much more I can tell you about her. She married Edward, and they had a baby daughter and went to live in Northumberland. I didn't see her for some years after that, not until after Edward had died, when the war was over."

They fell silent, disappointed and a little sad. Then Jane asked, "What happened to Marnie's baby?"

That had been a sad story, Gillie said. She was only five or six when the Second World War came, and she'd been sent away to America to be safe from the bombing. When she came back she was nearly thirteen, and seemed like another child, her mother said – so grown-up, and wilful, and independent. And she always seemed to bear her mother a grudge for having sent her away, even though it was for her own safety.

Gillie shook her head sadly. "They could never get on together after that, and yet Marnie had looked forward so much to having her back. Esmé used to say, 'How can I help it if I don't love you? I can't love you just *because* you're my mother. Anyway, you've never been a mother to me.' Oh, yes, she was terribly cruel, but in a way it was true. You see, Marnie tried to be a good mother to her – she wanted to be – but I don't think she knew how;

her own childhood had been so lonely and wretched...
And yet she'd always promised herself that her own
child should have everything she'd never had herself. As
it turned out – what with being sent away for six years
during the war, and her father being killed, she never had
the one thing she needed most – her own parents to love
her."

She stopped suddenly and glanced towards Anna,
then hurried on. "Anyway, she ran away and got married
as soon as she was old enough. Without even telling her
mother. That was why I said it was a sad story."

"Whose fault was it, then?" asked Jane, frowning at
the carpet.

"How can one say?" said Gillie. "When you grow as
old as I am you can't any longer say *this was someone's*
fault, and *that* was someone else's. It isn't so clear when
you take a long view. Blame seems to lie everywhere. Or
nowhere. Who can say where unhappiness begins?"

"You mean," said Jane, "that because Marnie wasn't
loved when she was little, she wasn't able to be a loving
mother herself, when her turn came?"

"Something like that," said Gillie. "Being loved,
oddly enough, is one of the things that helps us to grow
up. And in a way Marnie never grew up."

Jane turned to her mother. "According to that, Roly-
poly ought to be quite an old man by now, oughtn't he,
Mummy?"

They all laughed at that. Then Scilla said, "What happened to Esmé after that?"

She had married, Gillie said. He was a handsome fellow, black-haired and dark-eyed, but far too young and irresponsible. It hadn't been a happy marriage – though they'd had a baby, and Marnie'd hoped that might make the difference – but after a very short while it had ended in a divorce. But then Esmé had married again not long after and it had looked as if things might turn out happily after all.

"And didn't they?" asked Mrs Lindsay.

Gillie shook her head. "It was tragic, they were killed in a car crash on their honeymoon."

Anna felt Mrs Lindsay's knees stiffen behind her. She turned round. "That's funny," she whispered, "my mother was killed in a car crash too."

"I know," Mrs Lindsay whispered back, "your auntie told me." She pulled Anna gently back against her knees, then, speaking over her head, she said in a very quiet voice, "Gillie, what was the name of Esmé's baby?"

"She was called Marianna," Gillie said, "after her great-grandmother. Marnie was so pleased about that! And of course it *is* a lovely name. It had a Spanish sound about it too, which pleased the father."

Anna turned round to smile at Mrs Lindsay, as if to say, well, *that* couldn't have been me! But Mrs Lindsay was not looking at her this time. She was staring at Gillie, who was still talking to Jane and Scilla.

"Marnie adored that baby!" Gillie was saying. "You see, she had the looking after of her, right from when the first marriage broke up, so she was almost more hers than Esmé's. I think Marnie thought of the baby as her second chance. She was determined to make a good job of bringing her up."

"And did she?" asked Jane and Scilla eagerly.

"She didn't have her second chance after all," Gillie said quietly. "She never got over the shock of Esmé and her husband being killed. She was very ill after that, and she died later the same year. I was abroad when it happened so I'd lost touch. I wrote to the Northumberland address but never had a reply. And when I came back to Barnham I asked around, but of course nobody knew anything about the family by then, they'd left so long ago. There were strangers living in this house—" she broke off. Scilla sniffed. "Don't be too sad about it, my dears. It all happened a long time ago."

"How long?" asked Mrs Lindsay quickly.

"Six or seven years, I suppose," said Gillie, counting on her fingers.

"But what happened to the poor little girl?" asked Jane. "I hate a story without a proper ending."

There was a sudden movement behind Anna. She turned and saw Mrs Lindsay sitting bolt upright in her chair. Her eyes were shining and she was actually smiling.

Whose Fault Was It?

"Let me finish the story," she said, her voice quite shaking with excitement. "Yes, I can, though I didn't know I could until just now!" And she laughed at the surprised faces turned suddenly towards her.

Chapter Thirty-Six

THE END OF THE STORY

"THE END OF the story went like this," said Mrs Lindsay. "When her granny couldn't look after her any more, the little girl was sent away to a children's home. She was about three then. And a few years later a couple found her there. The woman had always wanted a daughter, because she hadn't one of her own, so they took Marianna back to their own home to live with them."

"Oh, I'm so glad!" sighed Jane.

Mrs Lindsay went on quickly, as if she were afraid of

being interrupted. "The woman loved her very much. She wanted her to call her 'mother', but for some reason Marianna never would. So she called her 'auntie' instead." Anna looked up, suddenly holding her breath. "And because the woman wanted so much to feel that the little girl was her own, she changed her name. At least, she didn't change it. She just used the last half."

There was a moment's silence, then Scilla burst out, "Anna! Mari-anna!"

"Do you mean it's *me*?" Anna said. "*Me*?"

"Yes, you," said Mrs Lindsay. "Are you pleased? Oh, Anna, I'm so glad! I think it's the loveliest ending to a story I ever heard – although I told it myself!"

She kissed Anna on the back of her head, and whispered in her ear, "So you see, the anchor did belong to you after all!"

Anna, feeling quite dazed, buried her head in Mrs Lindsay's lap for a moment. It was some minutes before they could all get over their surprise. Then everyone started asking questions at once. How had Mrs Lindsay known? And why hadn't she said so before? Why hadn't anyone told Anna that her granny used to live in The Marsh House? Didn't that make it almost more her house than theirs?

Mrs Lindsay agreed that it did although, of course, it did now belong to the Lindsays since they had bought it. But it certainly belonged to Anna's background more than to theirs.

Gradually the details came out. Mrs Lindsay had known no more than any of them, until that same afternoon when

Mrs Preston had told her all she knew about Anna's background. Even then she had no idea there could be any connection between Anna and the story of Marnie; not until Gillie had mentioned the car crash. After that it had all pieced together.

Mrs Preston had told her how she used to live near Little Overton herself, and how, years later, when she had been visiting the children's home, she had learned that the grandmother of the little girl she was interested in, had once lived there too. It had only come out by chance because the matron of the home had found a picture postcard of Little Overton among the child's possessions. It had been from her granny and had said on the back: *This is a picture of the house where I used to live when I was a little girl*.

Anna gave a little shiver of excitement. "I'm not saying anything your auntie didn't want me to say, you know," said Mrs Lindsay. "She asked me to tell you all this, and I was going to as soon as I had a chance."

"I know, she told me. Where's the postcard now?"

Mrs Lindsay explained that it had disappeared long since, even before Mr and Mrs Preston had come along. The matron had said the little Marianna wouldn't be parted from it and so it had eventually fallen to pieces. Anna looked disappointed, and Scilla said "O-oh," just as her mother had done earlier in the evening.

Mrs Preston had asked the Peggs once if they'd ever known a woman living on her own in the village with a three-year-old granddaughter, but they hadn't been able to think of anyone. And after all, it had said "when I was a little girl" – so Mrs Preston had put it in the back of her mind and tried to forget about it.

Andrew, arriving back in the middle of all this, was as excited as any of them. "But we haven't any *proof*," he said. "We can't be sure it was this house."

But there was another thing, Mrs Lindsay said. When Mrs Preston had come into the drawing-room, she had been astonished at the view. She hadn't realised the house was so near the water – having come by the road. Then later, when she was talking about the postcard, she said the matron had mentioned it was a big house by a lake. It hadn't struck Mrs Lindsay at the time that it could have been The Marsh House, photographed from the other side of the creek. She had thought she meant a big house somewhere inland, standing in its own grounds with a park. But just as Mrs Preston was leaving, she'd asked Mrs Lindsay whether she thought people ever had sailing boats on their own lakes. Mrs Lindsay had thought it rather a strange question, and asked why. Then Mrs Preston said the matron had mentioned a sailing boat in the picture as well. And she said something like, "I suppose it might have been one of the houses along here, mightn't it?"

"She had to hurry away then," said Mrs Lindsay, "so we had no more time to talk about it. But—"

"But there aren't any other houses along here," said Andrew. "Only the cottages."

"Exactly," said Mrs Lindsay.

They talked about it for hours. Gillie said Anna's grandmother must have told her many stories when she was little – "She was always a great talker!" she said – and she began wondering whether it was possible she could have told her the story about the beggar girl at some time; – it had been so odd Anna suddenly remembering about the sea lavender.

"But Anna was so little then," Mrs Lindsay said, and Gillie agreed.

But when Anna – struggling to find the right words – told them what she had never told anyone before – how The Marsh House had looked so familiar, like an old friend, even when she had first seen it, Gillie said, "Yes. Yes, of course. It would." If Anna had gazed at it long enough, (until it fell to pieces, in fact!) the picture would have remained in the back of her mind even after she had forgotten it. It was the same in painting, she said. You never forgot the places you painted out of doors, because you'd looked at them for so long that they seemed to become part of you.

And that reminded her… She had brought the painting she was doing on the marsh that day. It was really meant as a present for Mrs Lindsay, but she knew she wouldn't mind if…

Mrs Lindsay said, "Oh, no, what a lovely idea!"

The End of the Story

Then the painting was unpacked and given to Anna. It was The Marsh House, just as she had first seen it, with water coming right up to the foreground; the way it would look if you were standing with your feet in the water... Anna hardly knew how to say thank you, she was so pleased.

Then, when they were at last thinking of going to bed, Andrew suddenly said, "Oh, and I've got something for you too!" He produced a small parcel from his pocket and handed it to Anna with a bow.

"My lady Marianna, your toothbrush!"

Chapter Thirty-Seven

GOODBYE TO WUNTERMENNY

ANNA STOOD AT the window in The Marsh House, looking out on the staithe. It was nearly three weeks later, the weather was wet and windy, and most of the visitors had left. In two days' time she and the Lindsays would be going home too.

The staithe was deserted except for one small figure. She wiped the mist from the window, and saw that it was Wuntermenny, in his oilskins, just pushing off from the landing stage. Who but Wuntermenny would be going down to the beach on a day like this! she thought. It would be dreary down there, the sand pock-marked with rain, the stinging marram grass bent flat by the wind. She could picture him trudging along the shore, eyes and nose running, peering at pieces of wood, old sauce bottles, lumps of tallow, and stooping now and then to pick up some sodden treasure washed up by the waves. Dear old Wuntermenny who had eaten the sherbet bag! She must say goodbye to him. She might not see him again.

She slipped out of the room, unnoticed, and ran out of the side door.

Wuntermenny had passed the house already. She slid down the grassy bank, cut across the staithe, and scrambled up on to the dyke. Then she ran along it until she was nearly abreast of him.

"Wuntermenny!"

He turned and saw her.

"I'm going away!" she shouted. "Goodbye!"

The boat was carrying him steadily away from her. She could not tell if he had heard or not, but he cocked his head slightly towards her. She waved, then put her fingers to her lips and waved again. "I'm going away on Friday. Goodbye!"

She saw him lift his chin, as if to say "Oh, ah!" Then he raised his arm, and with a single wave that was more like a solemn salute, he disappeared round the bend.

Anna stood looking after him. The seagulls wheeled

and screamed overhead. The wind was whipping the water into small pointed waves, and the marsh, beyond the creek, looked grey and desolate. Now that Wuntermenny had gone, there was no single person in sight. In all the world there seemed to be no-one but Anna standing alone on the dyke under the huge, leaden sky.

She was glad she had said goodbye to him. He was the loneliest person she had ever known. And yet he had been one of eleven children! She had been lonely because she was one. And Marnie had been lonely because she was one.

It was raining harder now and she was beginning to get wet, but it did not matter. She was warm inside. She turned and began running back along the dyke, thinking how strange it was – about being 'inside' or 'outside'. It was nothing to do with there being other people, or whether you were 'an only', or one of a large family – Scilla, and even Andrew, felt outside sometimes; she knew that now – it was something to do with how you were feeling inside yourself.

In another two minutes she would be back in The Marsh House, sitting with all the others round the sweet-smelling, crackling wood fire, toasting her feet and having tea and toasted buns. But even then she could not be feeling more 'inside' than she was at this minute, running alone down the dyke, outside, in the wind and the rain.

The wind made a roaring noise in her ears as she ran, and she shouted and sang at the top of her voice. She remembered once, some summer morning – when had it been? – running along a dyke in a wind like this, and feeling the same sort of happiness. Then she remembered. It was when she had been with Marnie, that first time they had gone mushrooming – that first time they had been real friends.

She slithered down on to the staithe – the grass bank was too slippery to climb up – and danced along by the edge of the creek. A white seagull's feather came tossing and turning through the air and fluttered to her feet. She grabbed at it, before the wind should seize it again and carry it off – and looked up.

For an instant she fancied she saw someone – a little girl with long, fair hair – waving to her from one of the upper windows of The Marsh House. But there was no-one there. Only a curtain was blowing outwards and flapping in the wind. Scilla must have forgotten to shut the window. It was the end window – the window that had once been Marnie's... She stood for a moment, watching the rain falling slantwise across the house and streaming in rivers down the window panes, wondering what it reminded her of. Then she remembered that, too.

Mrs Lindsay was just bringing in the tea things when Anna came in at the side door. She looked horrified when she saw her.

"For goodness' sake!" she exclaimed. "You're drenched! What *have* you been up to? Have you been outside in all this?"

"Yes," said Anna, and she laughed. "But I'm inside now!"

"I should jolly well think you are," said Mrs Lindsay, looking at the trail of rainwater and wet footprints on the floor. And – as she said to her husband later, she hadn't the heart to scold her, she looked so absurdly happy.

"There was another thing," Mrs Lindsay told him. "The children were talking about Marnie when she came in – they just can't get over that story – and Matt was talking in his usual tactless way, saying something about it being sad for Anna, not having known her. And do you know what the child said? She said, 'I did know her once.' Quite definitely, just like that. Well, so she did, of course – when she was very little. But it was funny – she actually laughed when she said it, just as if she really remembered her.''

Postscript

As my mother is no longer here to tell you how she came to write about Marnie, I will tell you all I remember of the very beginnings of her story, and that summer holiday in a North Norfolk village.

Every year since I was a child, we spent our summer holidays in this village. Every day we would cross the salt marsh to our beach, an island of sandhills and marram grass. There we would bathe in the cold North Sea, then settle down in the hills for a picnic lunch. The same families used to come to the beach every day, like us. We each had our own pitch which we kept for many years – usually until a terrific storm washed the sandhill away into the sea. The children on the island used to gather together after lunch and go for walks along the beach, collecting driftwood to make a raft or digging channels and building dams to create pools, leaving the grown-ups to doze.

The year of Marnie was just the same, only I was grown up by then, and the children who gathered together to build sandcastles were the next generation of the same families.

One balmy evening, the sun glowing low in the sky, my mother was wandering home from the beach along the marsh path towards a small row of houses on the other side of the creek. The square black Watch House was on the right, and near to it stood The Granary, a long low comfortable-looking house of soft red brick with a blue door and windows. Everything was very still, the tide was out and the creek was almost deserted. Only the great black-backed gulls continued their squawking.

My mother stopped halfway along the path to watch some ducks plodding around in the mud. When she looked back, The Granary seemed to have disappeared; to have melted into the background. It was several minutes before the low rays of the sun struck the brickwork, making the house reappear.

At the end of the path, she crossed some sand and began to paddle across the creek. There in an upper window of The Granary was a little girl, sitting having her long fair hair brushed. This was the beginning of Marnie.

My parents still went to the island every day. After a bathe they would struggle up the soft sand into the sandhills, and here my mother would mull over the characters of Marnie and Anna, jotting down notes in a little black pocket book with a hard cover. She had vivid memories of how she felt as a child, and Anna in particular, with her 'ordinary' look and feelings of being on the outside, was very much drawn from her own childhood.

At the end of that summer my parents returned home. My mother, still jotting down notes, had already filled several notebooks and the story was emerging. She worked in a little shed in the garden, made comfortable with light and heat and nothing to distract her but birds or the occasional cat. Over the course of about eighteen months she progressed from notebooks to a clattering old typewriter, until the manuscript was finally ready to send to a publisher. My mother was delighted when the book was accepted, and her friend Peggy Fortnum agreed to illustrate it. But at the last minute she had to change the title from *Marnie* to *When Marnie Was There*, because Alfred Hitchcock was bringing out a film of that name just weeks before publication.

The book was a great success and was published in several languages. And in the summer of 1971, a BBC film crew came to the village to take photographs for the children's programme *Jackanory*. My mother wasn't able to be in Norfolk at that time, so my husband and I met the crew and showed them around. They auditioned many local girls and finally chose Marnie and Anna. I remember they dressed Marnie in a long white nightgown.

We had offered to help with the filming. So the first job they had for us was to get a couple of rowing dinghies – one to carry the director, and one to carry the photographer. I remember I had the photographer in my boat. As a fast-flowing spring tide was racing up the creek, I had to row like fury against it to keep the boat still for the photographer, who stood, precariously balanced, shooting Marnie at the edge of the creek with the sun in ribbons on the surface of the water. At the end of the week, the film crew treated us to a delicious meal in a local restaurant. I heard later that the photographer had won an award for his photographs of Marnie.

Thirty years after the book was published, I heard how a Japanese man had recently arrived in the village looking for 'Little Overton'. Many years before, as a young teenager, he had read *When Marnie Was There* in Japanese. The book had made a great impression on him and he very much wanted to see the place where the story was set.

It was the end of September and he had booked a tour from Japan to London for a few nights. He spoke very little English and he had no idea where 'Little Overton' was. All he had was a copy of the book as his guide. So he took the train to King's Lynn, as Anna had done; and finally caught the bus that goes along the coast. The bus was full of people, who were all very kind – but no-one knew where 'Little Overton' was. At each stop the passengers got off until he was the only person left. He began to get rather anxious. Then as the bus turned the corner he saw the windmill.

"Stop, stop!" he said, "This must be it!" And he leapt off the bus. But the village wasn't 'Little Overton', it was Burnham Overy.

He made his way to the pub. There the landlord assured him that he had found the right place, and took him down to the creek. He was thrilled to be there at last.

To see the tide rising, the boats swinging at anchor, the wild marsh and birds and the house that had been the start of it all.

That evening, while looking for somewhere to stay, he passed a house with a Japanese name. He met a lady there who could not only understand the story of his journey, but was also from the same place in Japan. She has since visited him there, taking him a photograph of my mother as a present.

Throughout her life my mother had strong ties with Norfolk. But since 1950 Burnham Overy in particular was special to her. So when she died in 1988, while on holiday, we arranged for her to be buried in the little churchyard of St Clement's; in the village that had inspired her to write not just this story but also her other novels: *Charley, Meg and Maxie* and *The Summer Surprise*.

It is now twelve years later and over that time more Japanese and other nationalities have visited the village to see the salt-marsh creek and the house where Marnie and Anna met.

Then in December 2013 the exciting news broke that Studio Ghibli had chosen *When Marnie Was There* to be made into a motion picture. My mother's story of the unloved and lonely Anna, a story so personal to her, which resonates with so many of all ages, will be brought to a new generation in a new form.

I keep thinking how surprised and pleased my mother would be. Of all of her books this is the one she loved the most.

DEBORAH SHEPPARD

April 2002, May 2014